MIMOUN

MIMOUN

RAFAEL CHIRBES

Translated by Gerald Martin

Library of Congress Catalog Card Number: 91-61208

British Library Cataloguing-in-Publication Data

Chirbes, Rafael
  Mimoun.
  I. Title
  863 [F]

  ISBN 1-85242-220-3

First published in 1988 by
Editorial Anagrama, Barcelona

This edition first published in 1992 by Serpent's Tail,
4 Blackstock Mews, London N4 and
401 West Broadway #2, New York, NY 10012

Set in 11$\frac{1}{2}$/15pt Bembo by Saxon Printing Ltd, Derby
Printed in Hungary by Egyetemi Nyomda

MIMOUN

1 When I took that hasty decision to live in Morocco I did not imagine that, in a country I had toured on several occasions and which had always seemed to be a desert, it could rain so much. And yet that winter I spent in Mimoun it rained for weeks at a time. The wind tore at the branches of the trees, and the branches, as they moved, tormented my imagination. They contrived with their mournful sound to stir up my emotions and carry me away to states of mind more appropriate to an adolescent than to the man I had become.

2   Fez, that first week of September, lay sick and dirty in a landscape of withered bushes. During the day the city seemed to burn in a heavy grey haze, and at night the moon, above the outline of hills dotted with tombs and olive trees, caught fire.

For someone as tired and depressed as I, it was almost impossible to negotiate the town's asphyxiating backdrop or wander in search of a teaching post through the hopeless offices of that university building, formerly a barracks, in whose courtyard cows grazed and chickens scratched. All I can remember of those first days in Fez is the clatter of the old taxis that took me to the university, the clinging dust and the sad grey leaves of the eucalyptus trees.

I had taken a room on the second floor of the Hotel Jeanne d'Arc and still hadn't dared to stretch out in that strange bathroom, through which enormous red cockroaches marched. I felt a mixture of fascination and disgust at the smell of urine, excrement and spices in the decrepit medina, which to me appeared some marvellous sanctuary closed to the stranger. I used to roam its winding streets as if, just by walking, I might find the clues which would unlock that world I imagined so mystical.

I went almost daily to see the four other Spanish teachers, who shared an apartment near the Jeanne d'Arc, in the decaying new part of town. I spent long hours with them on the terraces of boulevard cafés: the Zanzi-Bar, the Maroc, the Marignan. From there, behind our cups, we watched the peasants go by, the easy women, the opportunists fighting for a place in the civil service; but above all, we watched the time go by. Everything seemed so far away and incredible. As if the dilapidated colonial houses were just a filmset, and the people were extras in between takes. For us the city existed only as some interminable script, to which we added a new scene every day.

Before dinner I would leave the Spaniards and lose myself once more in the alleyways of the medina, beyond Bab Boujouloud, and wait for the time when the shop lamps began to give off that whitish light that hissed on copper and leather objects, on silver and piles of spices. I still thought Fez the most beautiful city in the world, though I could no longer have said why. As though a sea of sadness had flooded that sparkling labyrinth, as though things and people had been submerged beneath it, and were little by little fading and leaving pitiful trails of colour behind them.

At the beginning of October I finally managed to get a job, and yet I still didn't feel good. I felt it had come too late and I was no longer even sure I wanted to live in that dusty city. The smell of manure blotted out the perfume of spices and began to suffocate me, slowly, as I sat on the boulevard terraces.

3 I found that I had very few teaching hours each week and my classes required little preparation. I would have as much free time as I wanted; but this discovery, which would have been wonderful anywhere else, in Fez, imprisoned in the small circle of Spanish teachers, frightened rather than delighted me.

I had realised I could never live in the medina, in one of those magnificent old houses bereft of all comforts, especially when occupied by only one person. Nor was I seduced by the idea of renting an apartment in the new quarter and enveloping myself in some third-rate European life in hateful exile. I decided to leave for any other town in the surrounding region. The fact was that I had only to turn up to classes a couple of days a week, and although I had no car I could settle outside Fez without too much inconvenience. I considered Immouzzer, but Alcira, one of the Spaniards, put me off the idea: apparently in winter the road was frequently cut off by snow.

He it was who suggested Mimoun as an alternative place of residence, offering to take me in his car to get to know it. Moreover, there was a Spaniard living in Mimoun who, if I could reach an agreement with him, might share his house with me until I found one of my own.

In the last days of my stay in Fez I met Ahmed and finally made use of the immense bathroom in the Jeanne d'Arc, after we'd given it a thorough clean. I still don't know quite how Ahmed managed to sneak into the hotel each night and stay until morning without paying a cent. He had a glistening skin, like rubber, and lived in some unspecified house behind a bush of oleanders. He was the sort of Moroccan fascinated by European cars and blue jeans. He asked for his coffee in French and took up, with what he considered good taste, every topic circulating among the city's functionaries, like some revolting caricature of the worst idiocies passed on by the French aid workers.

– A Fes, le meilleur café c'est au Zanzi-Bar. Moi, j'adore le café du Zanzi-Bar. Je le prends toujours là.

There in the Zanzi-Bar he was greeted by older men who thought exactly as he did. I really couldn't bear that environment. It was about then that I began to understand that most café conversations involving middle-class Moroccans were about money. I learned the word 'flus' and I learned it was good form to play the *tiercé*. The radio stations carried direct broadcasts of the Longchamps races on Sunday afternoons, though I still can't work out where the men got the money to buy their bottles of Johnny Walker, which they drank in clapped-out cars where they would shut themselves away with some woman.

★

I could not fall in love with Ahmed, in spite of his body. I couldn't even bear him when we were in bed and gossiping our way round a city of acquaintances as trivial as he was. Little by little we stopped seeing each other. Probably Ahmed was as bored with me as I was with him. Besides, I was already preparing my escape to Mimoun. I'd made a brief excursion with Alcira, I had met Francisco, the Spaniard in Mimoun, and well, let's just say that Fez had ceased to interest me.

4 I arrived in Mimoun well into autumn, when the days were shorter and fresher, the first rains had fallen and the leaves on the trees were beginning to take on marvellous golden hues. It was a good start to find the earth damp and red, with the sky as clear as enamel. I was excited at the smell of burning wood, the purity of the air and the outline of the minarets sharp against the sky.

I had moved into Francisco's house, which everyone knew as La Creuse du Bon Dieu because it had been built next to a ravine with the aim of serving as a Catholic church and the house of a French missionary. The missionary, in his zeal to convert the Muslims, had chosen to build his mission-house at the edge of the road which led to the Marabout's hermitage situated at the very top of the hill, in which was kept the tomb of a miraculous holy man, Sidi Ahmed Al-Qarin, an object of veneration for the Muslim faithful.

The house, though none too comfortable, was a truly beautiful mansion with large domes and windows through whose panes one could view the tree-lined avenue, the small white town crowded beneath the minarets and the blue and mysterious line of the Atlas mountains, floating in the distance, suspended from the sky.

The first days were unforgettable. The leaves turned a deeper gold behind the window panes, and flocks of white birds hurried away to the south, filling the house with their melancholy calls.

One morning there was snow on the furthest reaches of the fantastic mass of Bou Iblan and the cold obliged us to light the stoves in our rooms, in an effort to fend off the wind which crept in through the cracked windows. The smell of burning wood invaded the inside of the house, everything seemed to shrink back even more around us, and that day we stayed gazing for hours at the countryside, waiting for the moon to rise on the horizon behind the vague snow-capped cordillera.

The moon appeared like some exquisite jewel.

Francisco gave classes at the local institute and did pencil drawings in large yellow sketchpads. He had been living in Mimoun for years, after some modest success in Spain as a sculptor. But shortly after his arrival he had given up sculpture and suffered whenever he happened to recall it.

"I came here to work in peace," he said, "and look at me. I know now I'll never go back to sculpting. This country burns you out."

He liked well planned scenes, so this verdict on his life would always coincide with a gesture which took the flame of a match to the tip of his hashish cigarette.

"The indolence of the Moroccan," he would say,

letting out the first puff of smoke and offering me the cigarette. "The indolence of the fucking Moroccan. In this country there's a virus no one escapes from. In the end, one becomes a Moor too."

He would get up and stand in front of me with his arms outstretched, as if someone had just crucified him. He was a martyred Christian. His fragile birdlike body was wrapped in a *gandora*.

"Don't you see? I'm more Moor than Spanish by now. There's nothing for me to do back there. I've dug myself a grave I can't escape from."

His eyes glistened as if he'd started to cry. He glided over to the record player on his huge yellow slippers, and then went over to the east-facing window, which opened on to the town, the plain and the unsettling outline of the Atlas mountains. In the half light of the early evening, the moon was already sailing above the hills.

"Here, at least, I have this!" he said, stretching his hands towards the glass of the window. "This peace. This marvellous moon. Come. Come and see."

He led me over to the window, offered me another drag on the dying cigarette and made me gaze at the moon, which seemed to be pointing at us with its silver horns. The room, with the record player at full blast, was filled with drumming and Berber cries, the fire trembled in the grate and all the wood and copper objects bought in far-off southern souks seemed to grow unaccountably larger.

It was dinner time. Opposite the house the lights

had come on in a nearby dwelling which in its day had belonged to the missionary's servant and was now occupied by a strange Frenchman who barely moved his head to greet us.

"For a long time I thought Charpent was dumb!" Francisco said. "Later I found out he wasn't. He teaches in a private school in Fez. One day, as he passed me in the street, he let out an alarming sound, as if someone had just kicked him in the stomach. It's the closest he's come to articulate speech."

He scarcely had any visitors. Sometimes he would appear with a couple of unpleasant men and two girls who looked like prostitutes. He would shut himself away for hours, and the sound of vulgar music would come drifting across from his house. The visitors would leave in the early morning making a hell of a racket. Then, for weeks at a time, no one would visit Charpent, who would park his car – almost furtively – near the door and go inside without raising his eyes. Francisco and I were convinced that during these long periods he used to drink alone. His face was covered in red blotches and scales. We both felt sorry for him. Francisco was frightened by him as well.

"He's so mysterious," he said. "Have you noticed his eyes?"

I had not had a chance to see them up to then.

5 My work turned out to be a doddle. I went down to Fez for my classes only twice a week, using the communal taxis. The rest of the time I spent in Mimoun, hardly leaving the house. I read, worked on the final drafts of the novel I'd started in Madrid and filled my head with ideas for a new one. I'd stopped drinking: all I took was the mint tea prepared for us by Rachida, the woman who came each day to do the cleaning.

Everything was in order. Francisco made plans as to how we should see to the garden when the spring came, whilst I spent all my time thinking about finding a house of my own. I was longing to start enjoying that independence whose quest had taken me to Mimoun. Besides, I had a feeling that happiness could not last too long.

Sometimes we would come across Ahmed wandering by the taxi rank in Fez, by Atlas Square. We would sit on one of the benches, beneath the enormous jacarandas, or have something in the Atlas Café, which didn't please Ahmed because he thought it rather inelegant.

I found its mirrors beautiful, with their peeling silver and the little black flecks the flies left everywhere. Those mirrors, when spring came, would reflect the blue jacaranda flowers, which seemed to bloom out of the morning mist, hanging from the still bare trees. In Morocco I soon fell in love with that tree whose flowers appear before its leaves.

The unexpected meetings with Ahmed would end up in one of the rooms of the Jeanne d'Arc. Today I have melancholy memories of the tap that filled the strange bathtub with warm water and the steam that rose from the water until it filled the room. Ahmed's naked body appeared out of the steam just as, in spring, in Atlas Square, the blue jacaranda flowers would bloom out of the mist.

Some evenings, back in Mimoun, before beginning the walk up to La Creuse, I would stop in one of the bars for a drink. My presence in that out of the way city caused a mixture of curiosity, sympathy and suspicion. Years before, Mimoun had been an important commercial centre but had fallen into gradual decline. The French had moved out the day after independence and the last Jews had left the city when the Yom Kippur War broke out. There were just a couple of them left, owners of liquor stores and much reviled.

When I arrived in Mimoun, the French quarter, with its art deco villas, was almost abandoned. The most elegant houses had been occupied by wealthy Moroccans who ruined the old architecture to adapt it to their own way of life. Other villas grew old and deserted among gardens which had been magnificent in their day but were now overrun by weeds. Among the bushes there still stood magnificent ornamental trees, like remnants of the former splendour.

On the other hand, in the heart of the decaying medina, what once had been a flourishing *mellah* had turned into the red light district, drunken soldiers urinated in the alleyways and bedbugs reproduced themselves in silence beneath the covers of straw mattresses. Mimoun was a dead town which only came to life during the Thursday souk, when the Berbers from the local countryside besieged it with their asses, their sheep and goats, and their baskets full of eggs.

I believe the decrepitude of the town was passed on to its inhabitants, and that the peeling walls of the cafés communicated mysteriously with the wrinkles in the clothes of the customers. That decrepitude gradually took hold of my soul, my bouts in the local bars became prolonged, and each day the climb up to the house grew harder.

Without even noticing it, I had gone back to drinking as I did in Madrid, and I stayed for long hours propping up the bars, where I received new offers of friendship each day and had frequently to escape from invitations which did not entice me. Despite myself, I had become the novelty of that autumn in the dead town, which was enlivened only by the soldiers in the nearby barracks.

Francisco didn't like me drinking with Moroccans. "They don't know how to drink. They just turn nasty," he said, "and you land up getting yourself in one big mess." I think he was afraid I would start taking my new friends back to the house. He was scared of losing his hard won intimate relationships. He preferred to go up at sunset to a café close to the Marabout, where the young locals hung around and sang. Up there, the smoke from the kif brought the adolescents and the soldiers from the barracks into ambiguous proximity.

My drinking companions disapproved of the Marabout Café, and always spoke of it with disdainful smiles and giggles in allusion to things no one would explain to me, but which I could imagine. Almost without trying, Francisco and I had contrived not to get in each other's way by inserting ourselves into separate worlds with no contact between them.

Around that time I came to realise that no one in Mimoun would have agreed to live in the house we inhabited. There was a mystery about it and it had been marked by a curse. Apparently – so they told me in the bar – the Muslim faithful had avenged themselves on the missionary who had tried to take them away from their own religion and their veneration for Sidi Ahmed Al-Qarim and had succeeded, using complicated arts, in driving him mad.

"For months he howled every night like a dog, and his howls reached the very door of the Marabout, terrifying the pilgrims."

He had been abandoned. The servant left the nearby dwelling which Charpent would later occupy, and the faithful who climbed up to visit the holy man preferred to take the long way round rather than approach the accursed house. Only dogs roamed beneath the closed windows, attracted perhaps by the howls of the missionary. Little by little, silence fell and an intolerable stench took hold of the ravine. In the end the dogs could no longer control their anxiety, went crashing in through the windows, and installed themselves in the house. Days later, the gendarmes found the priest's head hanging from a rope in the middle of the drawing room. The rest of the body, up to the shoulders, had been eaten by the dogs.

6 When I learned of the former owner's fate, I became afraid of the dogs which roamed around the house. I came across them – threatening or fearful – as I climbed the hill after my habitual tour of the bars. On nights when I had drunk too much I used to bellow to scare them off and then, the next morning, I would be embarrassed at the thought that someone might have been listening to my cries.

The rains had started in Mimoun, and it was good to be indoors listening to the sound of the drops landing on the roof and on the window panes. Francisco had found an old piano and some folders of musical scores, and spent the day playing pieces by Satie, Schubert and Chopin. In addition, we had a good collection of classical records, some books and the woman who came each morning to cook our meals and keep things tidy.

The earth in Mimoun was red in colour, and although I had bought myself some boots which came halfway up my calves, my trouser legs were always splashed with mud. The road to the house was turned periodically into a mudslide, which the dogs crossed like fugitive shadows. I used to watch them splashing through the puddles beneath the yellow lights and at night they barked endlessly outside the house. The winter cold had worn down the grass on the open space which served as a garden and separated La Creuse from Charpent's place. Whenever it stopped raining for a day or two, I would hear the sound of dogs' paws on the dry grass during the night. Sometimes the noise would keep me awake, other times it got into my nightmares.

I used to dream about dogs invading the garden and I could hear their steps from the bedroom. One of them, particularly large and dirty, scratched around in the grass and ran, with menacing steps, ever closer to the window. Little by little, the walls of the room became transparent and I could see him looking into the room, as if he intended to leap in at any moment. I would shout out to frighten him; I wanted him to know that the house was not empty; that he should not come in. I shouted with all my might, but no sound came from my lips. The dog finally jumped through the glass and the closed shutters, which gave way without resistance, gently and in silence. He would move then to my side, very close, until I could feel his warm, damp breath on my face. It was useless to go on shouting because I could not make a single sound, though I could hear him panting in my ear and feel his tongue starting to lick my helpless lips.

Once I woke in time to hear my own shout, the one I could never hear in my dreams. Then I found Francisco, kneeling beside the bed.

"You were snarling, in your sleep, as though you were a dog," he said, "and you were clawing at the straw cover beneath the mattress.''

That's how I discovered that I myself was the dog that pursued me in the night. I started to laugh, and got up to have a cigarette with Francisco. Despite my laughter, my breathing was accelerated by my fear.

Francisco had begun to play something by Satie on the piano, as subtle as a solitary whispered monologue which scarcely disturbed the silence of the night. I thought of the former owner of those folders. What kind of life must he have led in Mimoun. And for how long. Francisco had acquired the folders in the local *funduk:* a run-down store which the shepherds and Berber peasants used as a stable when they came down to Mimoun for the Thursday souk. Stored in that place, alongside the asses, sheep and goats, there were broken boxes, old wrought iron stoves of exquisite design, and fine, albeit battered pieces of furniture built in the same style as those adorning the finest houses in Paris or London back in the twenties and thirties.

Amongst the wretched bric-à-brac from the *funduk*, Francisco had acquired his piano, his scores and some of the pieces of furniture scattered about the rooms of the house. There was a gigantic mahogany bookcase, almost empty, which took up the whole of one of the interminable walls, as though it had been made to measure; and the table which Francisco had chosen for the drawing room was also of such a size that it could only have found a place in a house like that.

Whilst I smoked my cigarette, sitting beside the piano on the cushions we had scattered around the floor, I was seized with the certainty that most of the second-hand objects Francisco had collected together were made to occupy exactly the place they now occupied, and that even Satie's music had adapted to that space as if it were used to living in it.

Francisco had stopped playing, smoothed out his slender hands, all of whose bones protruded, and smiled.

"How goes it, dog-man? Are you feeling better, or is the music bothering you?"

I told him it wasn't bothering me, and he took the chance to talk, as he had on previous occasions, of the beauty of Satie's music and the charm of those winter nights when wandering clouds cross the sky like ghost ships which sometimes hide the moon and leave the world more silent than before.

"Here, smoke this."

He handed me a hashish cigarette and began to play again. He looked like a bird, bent over the piano, so frail with his sparse tousled hair and his sharp nose. I felt sorry for him then, wrapped in the cellophane of his innocence, caressing, as he turned them, those poisoned pages. I thought that I should never tell him the legend of the missionary who had tried to conquer the soul of Mimoun. I looked at the great table, the mahogany bookcase and the windows which the night had turned opaque.

"I don't know why," I said, "but dogs have always frightened me. And there are so many around here."

7 Anyone could have died of boredom in the University of Fez. The students thought of nothing but the prospect of finding a job as soon as possible, to support their entire family with a government salary. Until that day, they lived out a sordid existence in the university blocks, where they occupied poorly ventilated rooms full of clothes hanging to dry and dirty saucepans. Most of the inhabitants of the so-called University City were on State grants, almost all of which they sent to families prostrated by misery in lost villages whose names were not written on any map and through which no road passed.

The French lecturers – who dominated the Spanish Department – wanted only to save a few thousand francs a month, with the hope of setting up some family business on their return to the home country, or of purchasing some rural property which they would furnish with the copper pieces and tapestries they sent back each year. The few Moroccans who gave classes in the department confined themselves to showing off at the counters of boulevard cafés and acquiring bottles of whisky to drink with their female pupils. They spoke in a Spanish closer to Millán Astray than to Cervantes, could not disguise their sense of inferiority in the presence of

Europeans, and entertained themselves by telling dirty stories.

"Tu vois la plus petite? Celle du blue jeans? Je l'ai tapée l'autre nuit. On était six à la chambre et on a bu quatre bouteilles de whisky. Les trois filles, provenantes des meilleures familles de Fès, étaient, toutes les trois, nues."

We Spaniards found it hard to tolerate that barracks atmosphere, which we tried to frequent as little as possible and from which only one of the local teachers managed to escape, a new arrival with an interest in Spanish literature and a strange pride in being Moroccan. His name was Abd-el-Jaq, or Slave of the True One, which seemed to me as beautiful as his bearing.

We became good friends almost as soon as we met. I started to lend him some of the few books I had brought to Mimoun with me, and others which had arrived later, sent by friends back in Spain.

I would stay to chat to Abd-el-Jaq after work and we got in the habit between classes of visiting the stalls set up in the university corridors by the janitor, where they sold boiled eggs with cumin, hard bread and glasses of mint tea. I invited Abd-el-Jaq back to our house in Mimoun, even though I was not at all convinced that Francisco would be pleased at the visit and feared that things would end in some tremendous misunderstanding.

When Abd-el-Jaq finally came to Mimoun, he refused to visit the house at La Creuse. "Another time", he said, and searched out my little finger with his. The taxi had stopped at the garden of Bab Marwan, by the gate in the wall. Despite the cold, the children were playing on the esplanade, fighting against the first shadows of the night. The radio had broadcast a news bulletin, and then the perfect voice of Um Kultum boomed out, as we plunged, hand in hand, into the sordid streets of the *mellah*. We had a tea to keep out the cold before stopping at a house with its shutters painted the colour of dried blood. There Abd–el–Jaq chose a dyed redhead, with black teeth and wrinkled hands. I took a girl with dark skin and short curly hair, who can't have been more than sixteen and looked like the Sumurrut whom Pasolini chose for his *Arabian Nights*. She was so beautiful I was almost afraid to touch her, but when she undressed her sex gave off an unbearable stench.

We lay down on two straw mattresses almost side by side, and whilst I embraced the foul-smelling Sumurrut, I could hear the gasps of Abd–el–Jaq and saw his buttocks opening and closing every time he penetrated the woman with the red hair.

I have always thought that the woman who turned to look at us as we left the brothel was Rachida, and that this was the day when she began to treat me as an accomplice whenever Francisco tormented her with his manias. The truth is that outside the house I never recognised Rachida. She covered her face with a black veil and wrapped her body in a cream-coloured kaftan, identical to those worn by most other women of her age.

She was not old, though her face was full of wrinkles and most of her original teeth had been replaced by bits of metal. Only her arms were still clean, white and firm.

When we met on the road up to La Creuse, she would pause to gaze at me and greet me joyfully.

"Manuel!"

Sometimes I almost bumped into her without recognising her. She would stop in front of me and smile from behind the veil.

"Est-ce que tu ne me reconnais pas?"

For her those meetings were a game from which she always emerged the winner. She was amused at my clumsiness, so European, and the fact that I never recognised her. Moroccans did not need to see a woman's face to know her. They noticed details that still eluded me, some of which I slowly learned. For Rachida, we Nazarenes were strange people, like immature children who had grown up in some unnatural way. Sometimes I think we just seemed plain stupid to them.

Rachida had learned to obey Francisco quite blindly and satisfied his every whim in the way you satisfy a spoiled child. I think her opinion of Europeans derived in large measure from her dealings with him. With me she began to adopt a slightly different attitude, perhaps after she had seen me leave the brothel in the company of Abd-el-Jaq; or because on other occasions she had seen me roaming the bars accompanied by people she knew from Mimoun. For Rachida I was an ambiguous specimen, already capable of some insights, albeit on a limited number of subjects: something like an embryonic Moroccan successfully following the process of evolution.

That would explain why she smiled at me behind Francisco's back each time he ordered her to do things she found inappropriate in a mature person: whenever he missed classes for a few days he stayed in bed and asked her to put the table by the headboard and serve him his meals there in the room. At those times Rachida would look at me with pity because I too had to eat in the room, pandering to Francisco's whims. She smiled as one slave smiles at another.

Francisco spent weeks at a time in bed. From there he nurtured his mysterious inner life. He followed the trajectory of the sun and the moon, the colour variations of the leaves on the trees and the play of light and shadow on the surfaces of the furniture. At times I would hear him weeping and at others I would find him in a feverish state, drawing in his yellow sketchpads bodies in movement and faces he had seen somewhere. He would lie silent for hours and then, suddenly, start shouting because the stove was beginning to smoke, or because there wasn't enough wood in the large basket beside the burner; at other times he would complain that everything around him was frozen and he had lost the desire to go on living.

"I can't stand this country any longer," he would say. "Everyone. Everyone here deceives you."

For years he had waged an insane hand to hand struggle against an entire nation.

At night I used to hear him get up and stir the pots in the kitchen, or look for something in the drawing room. He would sigh – on purpose, I think – when he passed my room. I pretended to be asleep. His manias had begun to weary me, and I have to say that the days when Francisco shut himself in and the huge house fell silent came as a welcome relief. It was not proving easy living with him.

His confinements would end as unexpectedly as they began. Suddenly, one night, one would hear some piece of music on the piano and the voice of Francisco intoning some absurd invented lyric. It was the signal that alerted the other inhabitant of the house, the whole of nature, and a country which tortured him for no reason, to the fact that Francisco had just come back to life.

The following morning, as soon as Rachida arrived at the house, Francisco would get her to prepare a celebration dinner and so began a commotion which would last until nightfall. The furniture changed position and the tapestries which had decorated the walls until that moment would disappear and be replaced by others brought from who knows where. Francisco's house was a store with which I was barely acquainted. It was full of old suitcases, trunks and dusty corners piled high with wooden planks, weavings and half-finished sculptures.

"Rachida," trilled Francisco, "put lots of raisins in the couscous. And buy some flowers to liven up the drawing room and my bedroom. Would you like flowers in your room, Manuel? I've seen nothing but misery for a whole month now. I want to do something happy. I need it. And what other pleasures can one have in this country? I want to enjoy the things I couldn't have in Spain. Do you understand?"

Rachida obeyed him in everything. She bought flowers and did not spare the raisins in the couscous. It was a day of abundance during which other, sad days were negated, the ones when Francisco had shouted at Rachida for buying too much.

"Don't you see, we throw all that food away? You Moroccans think we Europeans are rich," he used to say. "But I'm not French. I'm a Spaniard and in that lousy institute I earn the same as a Moroccan and I don't even have enough money to go and see my family!"

That first time Rachida had wept, though without much conviction. Gradually she became used to the fact that one day would be like that and the next there would be an abundance of meat for the couscous and half the week's budget would go on roses.

When Francisco took the decision to get up from bed, it was because he had convinced himself once more that Morocco was marvellous and that all those people, including the ones he didn't know, were offering the best of themselves, though he couldn't think how to thank them. Francisco was unfamiliar with in-between feelings and would leap easily from the role of victim to that of executioner. Both suited him equally well.

"They are so noble, so ingenuous," he would say, and to prove it he would remember some anecdote he had lived out in some distant village, by some forgotten road; and he persuaded himself that everything around him was drawn with the same perfection as the human bodies in his yellow sketchpads: the tree-lined avenue that zig-zagged down to the town along the edge of the ravine, the great mass of Bou Iblan, buried beneath a mantle of snow, and the clear sky of the last day of autumn in the Atlas mountains.

When night fell, driven no doubt by the desire to make perfection still more perfect, Francisco would vanish from the house. I think he went up to the Marabout Café and stayed there singing and smoking with the adolescent boys until the early morning. Later, from my bedroom, I would hear muffled whispers and a gentle music that mingled with the creaking of the spring mattress.

8 Contrary to what Francisco thought, Charpent turned out to be a delightful fellow. I had the chance to meet him one day when it was pouring with rain and I was getting soaked beneath an umbrella that was of little use against the downpour. Charpent's face, behind the window of the car that had just halted alongside me, shone from beneath the flood with the hopeful light of certain biblical passages.

He drove me into Fez and, once there, refused to drop me in Atlas Square. Despite my protests, he took me right to the door of the faculty. On the way we spoke little; enough however for me to notice that he stammered and that this disability embarrassed him.

"A quelle heure est-ce que vous allez sortir cet après-midi?" he asked before driving away. I rejected the offer.

However, as I left after my class, I again came across Charpent's old yellow Renault parked opposite the faculty, as if it had not moved from there all day.

I suggested a beer before driving back up to Mimoun, and he accepted. We drank a dozen beers each in a bar owned by a Jewish woman, near Fez Boulevard. It was a ghastly place. The music was too loud and the drunks jostled, held hands, or kissed one another on the cheek, shouting as though each beer was the last of their lives. By the time we left the bar it was nightfall. I don't know how the time could have passed so quickly because Charpent didn't say much. He drank his beers in one go, Moroccan-style, and hummed to the songs that came over the loudspeakers.

Charpent liked poetry. I'd realised this when I met him at the door of the faculty, sheltering from the rain in his car: when he saw me he'd stretched out his hand and had let fall onto the back seat a copy of *Capitale de la Douleur* which he'd been reading until I knocked on the window to attract his attention. In the Jewish woman's bar, whilst we drank all those beers tasting of soapy water, he told me he'd published a couple of books of poetry back in France.

"Mais, de tout ça, il fait déjà quelque temps. On dirait que tous ces souvenirs appartiennent à une vie antérieure qui s'est tout à fait évanouie."

He drove as if hypnotised by the sweep of the windscreen wipers. He was drunk and stuttered even more than in the bar. I too was quite drunk, though I could have gone on drinking all night. I was thirsty and listened to Charpent as from a great distance, as though he were indeed speaking to me from the bottom of that now vanished former life. Everything was soft and distant.

The road too was erased beneath the night, and the rain. I felt weary, sleepy: whether tired or scared I didn't know – *"las ou lâche,"* Charpent had just said – watching the road go by and feeling time like a river beneath my feet, a road running away towards a destiny that was as unpredictable as it was absurd.

"Des livres, des mots. Je ne sais pas ce que je suis venu foutre ici, dans ce misérable trou. Je ne sais pas ce qui m'y retient encore. Maintenant, je suis malade. Vous savez? C'est Rilke qui l'a dit: 'Ô Seigneur, donne à chacun sa propre mort.' Mais vous le connaissez, bien sur."

The countryside, in the night, was like a sea rising up around the car. Mimoun was a step away. In the distance, the lights of Batij were shining through the mist on the slope of a black wave. Soon we would enter Plantain Boulevard, and would cruise beneath the whitish skeletons of the leafless trees, like the carcasses of phosphorescent whales in the fearful shipwreck that would end up carrying everything away. A dog ran in front of our headlights, and Charpent stopped the car, opened the door and staggered off into the dark. I heard him vomit beneath the rain, and then the heavy sound of his urine mingled with the splash of the water. I too got out to urinate and made a vain attempt to throw up, thinking that the anguish that had invaded me was due only to the fact that the beer had upset my stomach.

"Les chiens. Je les hais," said Charpent, as he went back to the car.

The rain was running across his forehead as though it were sweat.

"It's not tiredness," I thought, "it's cowardice, fear."

The yellow lights of Mimoun had begun to surround us and I had the impression they were asking something of Charpent, Francisco and me; something that only the crazy old missionary had given them.

9 I was writing so little. During the last weeks I had added no more than a few lines to the book; instead of writing, I cut and corrected. It was a task I carried out reluctantly, without optimism. My times at the typewriter grew shorter and more irregular. I felt tired, sleepy and thirsty; besides, after several months in Morocco, I had ceased to believe in the story it had seemed so important to tell when I was living in Madrid.

Madrid was an insignificant dot on the map, and my book was something lost in some invisible corner of that dot. I had got into the habit of reading in bed and I was drinking too much.

Each day I resolved not to set foot in the bars of Mimoun, where I was surrounded by people I disliked who were beginning to inspire in me a feeling very like fear. Nevertheless, come nightfall, I could not bear to stay indoors, whilst the shadows from the windows grew longer on the walls and the light became more fragile, like glass. At those times I would feel that I had just lost another day. I could not have explained to anyone how they might distinguish those lost days from others that might be won, but there, in La Creuse, once Rachida had gone, I began to feel unnerved.

I had to search for hope outside, beyond the corpses of the banana trees, the ruined houses of the colonial quarter, and the polished glass of the bars. What kind of hope could one find in there?

There were times when the solitude of La Creuse frightened me. Other times I would hear the sound of the door opening in a special way that I knew perfectly. Francisco inserted the key more carefully and pushed the door trying not to make any noise as it opened. This meant he had not returned alone and my presence was being tacitly warned off the drawing room and even more off Francisco's bedroom. We had never spoken about how I was to behave on those occasions, but we both knew it had to be like that.

I would stay in my room and try not to make a noise with my typewriter. It was necessary for the house to remain in silence, waiting for the obsessive sound of the Berber music to begin, like a ritual sacrificial chant. I would hear the cries and wails of the musicians, to which would be added the voices of Francisco and his companion. It was always the same: the Berber song taking possession of the silent house, the steam from the tea and the smoke of the hashish drifting invisibly beneath the doors, rounded off by the moans that floated through the air above the irritating sound of the mattress springs.

It was all as monotonous as my footsteps down to the town, searching for I know not what. At first I had arrived convinced I was looking for someone; many months had to pass before I realised I was already running away.

I had learned to mistrust smiles and invitations. I sensed that someone I did not know was casting an invisible net around me, a net which was growing ever larger, enveloping the smiles, the backslaps and all those glasses of soapy beer.

They bought me too many drinks and asked me too many questions. I had soon realised that at those sticky counters I would meet only police informants in search of an explanation for my presence in that desolate town, halfway between the world and the Sahara; or alcoholics who bloodied their hands on broken glasses and sang, fought and kissed, with a sour smell which they were gradually passing on to me. I knew that when they took that short journey across the frontier of misery, they usually ended up down by the river. There they drank alcohol mixed with water, until they found the relief of madness or death.

"Ah! L'Espagne! Et c'est Madrid que vous habitiez avant Mimoun? Vous n'avez pas bien choisi, monsieur."

The alcohol made my relationship with Francisco even more difficult. He couldn't stand me going ever more often to those bars. Sometimes he would make tense jokes when he saw me arrive home drunk. The more usual thing was for him to give me a hostile look and end up losing his temper, using any other reason as a pretext. The last argument we had – which made me decide to look for another house without delay – was because of Charpent.

Francisco became unbearable when I told him the Frenchman had taken me to Fez in his car, that we'd been drinking until late and that I'd invited him to choose a day to come and eat with us. It was as if I'd violated some especially sacred pact which had existed, until that moment, between the two of us.

"I don't want him in our house. That guy brings bad luck and he's not going to set foot in here. If you want to invite him, you can invite him to your house, the day you get it."

I don't know what insult I shouted before walking out, slamming the door, determined to return only to collect my things. I reserved a room in the local tavern and went drinking until they closed the last bar. It was raining torrentially; everything was soaked and smelled. It smelled of sodden djellaba wool. The mud spattered everything: my shoes, trouser legs, anorak. Drunk, I almost fell over several times. I was so afraid of being alone that night that I ended up looking for a prostitute. She followed me to the hotel door, drawn by the labels on a pair of wine bottles that I'd taken the precaution of hiding in my anorak. The night porter didn't see the labels, but with that sagacity characteristic of the sons of colonised peoples he detected the shape of the two bottles beneath the raincoat. I had to leave him a tip and a measure of wine before he would let us in. The whore, who was even drunker than I was, spent the night offering to pluck my pubic hair, according to Moroccan custom, and begging me to invite her to eat *jaluf* in my house, as if bacon was an indispensable accessory for playing the erotic game.

"Laisse-moi tranquille. Je n'ai pas de maison," I said.

She started to cry with the last glass of wine, and went on crying and protesting until dawn. She didn't know any French and couldn't understand any of the explanations I tried to give her. In the end she fell asleep, curled up like a little girl, with her head against my navel.

"Il faut attendre à demain," I began to sing, as if I were a nanny. "Demain, Inshallah, tu auras ton petit bout de jalouf, et moi, j'aurai une grosse et belle maison. Est-ce que tu veux aussi un beau jardin, ma princesse?"

The rain fell on the town like an insult. The first grey lights of the morning bathed the labels on my two empty bottles in sadness as they lay there on the floor. There was no sun that day.

10 The rain unfolded all the sadness of Morocco, lifted up its sick entrails and laid them out on the mud-encrusted stalls of the markets, the impassable roads and the cafés that stank of wet wool and dirt. Afterwards, quite suddenly, the rain turned to snow and seemed to purify us all. A peaceful silence fell over the abandoned gardens. It was as if, after a long illness, some old friend had come to visit us. The roads were lined with mute white flowers. The taxis from Bab Marwan carried their human cargo away towards Fez, and the peasants watched them go from behind the grimy windows of the Café de la Poste.

I found out later that Francisco too had spent the day behind the window panes of his room, watching the road to La Creuse, in case I returned. Rachida did not go in to work and in my room the firewood was burning, with its gentle moan, awaiting me.

I did not want to go back. I arranged to stay at the house of one of my habitual bar companions, whose name was Hassan and who worked as a technician in a rural development on the outskirts of Mimoun. I spent the day drinking with him and at night we slept together in a freezing room. Before we went to bed, completely drunk, we stood and kissed beside the straw mats. The room smelt damp and our breath was rank with sour beer. When I woke up, I saw that he was masturbating and I masturbated, too, in silence, beside him. We said not a word to each other. It was as if neither of us was aware of what the other was doing.

Francisco went down to Fez to tell the other Spaniards that we'd had a row and I had disappeared. Fortunately the other Spaniards didn't take much notice. So he decided to look for me in the Jeanne d'Arc, where they told him they'd never heard of me. In Morocco they forget a foreigner's name before his vices.

On his way back to Mimoun, Francisco went to the hospital, where a French doctor friend of his told him the same as the Moroccans in the Jeanne d'Arc, that he'd never heard of me. By then the night was falling, and Francisco – as he would tell me days later – had thought he was going mad. The snow had imposed a deathly silence on the city and the streets were deserted.

"I felt alone," he would later explain. "As if everything around me had disappeared. I was exhausted, I'd gone two nights without sleep, and I couldn't imagine where you'd got to. For a moment I came to think that destiny had been preparing everything for me to die alone in La Creuse."

They could have told him in the Mimoun tavern that I'd been there; or he could have got some information in the bar. However such a logical route would never enter Francisco's head. He had to end up presenting himself in the only place that any sensible person would avoid in Morocco. Francisco – who was capable of making every possible mistake – presented himself, asking after me, in the police station.

They made him wait a long time in a dilapidated hall, in which the only furniture was a giant portrait of His Majesty. They kept him standing, half-dead with cold, "and watching me, no doubt, through some crack," as he told me later.

He had been seen by an insinuating guy who – thanks to Francisco's intervention – would turn into my shadow for several months. We disliked one another from the first day. He appeared in Hassan's house after his interview with Francisco. He arrived with a couple of boys about ten years old, who played with the younger children of the family throughout his visit. I never did find out precisely what it was he suspected.

"Vous ne savez pas que votre copain vous cherche partout?" he asked. And then: "Les gens, au Maroc, sont trop polis, vous le saviez? Même les familles trop modestes pour supporter des invités, se taisent même si, parfois, on les dérange. Vous me comprenez?"

I had understood before that thin yellow-eyed guy had spoken a word to me. Hassan's family were not pleased at the presence of the police in their house and I was the cause of it. The fellow was warning me of what, no doubt, he had already warned the other members of the household. For some reason my presence there should be avoided. Hassan smiled at the policeman and offered him another glass of tea. I sensed that he was dying of fright.

11 I went back to La Creuse and, for the first time, wanted to return to Madrid. Once more the house beneath the rain and the road that curved by the front door. The rain dissolved the snow and uncovered the heaps of rubbish in the gutters. The light above the front door of the house was switched on in the middle of the day. The stray dogs lay slumped in silence at the foot of a dead acacia. They were soaking wet and didn't even turn to look at me. The French missionary's house. It was raining, and the rain somehow underlined the way the whole country smelled like a cemetery. Morocco. The endless cemeteries beneath the rain. The nameless tombs dug in the direction of Mecca. The corpses beneath the earth, decomposing amidst tears of rain.

I sensed Francisco peeping from behind one of the drawing-room windows. Then I thought not, that the house was empty and dead behind the needlessly lighted lamp. The geometrical outline of its walls marked a border. I was arriving from elsewhere, from an outside world in which bar counters and piles of rubbish grew at the roadsides. I was so tired I didn't even have the strength to call on him to open the door.

It wasn't locked. Beyond the walls everything was waiting. It was cold in the drawing room; neither of the two burners had been lit. I heard noises in

Francisco's room. It was him, waiting, like a hunter. I went straight to my room; there the fire was burning silently, and it was even a little too warm.

"Where have you been?" he said, after quite some time, no longer able to resist checking the nets he had cast.

"Fucking," I said, and he pretended he hadn't heard.

"Your clothes are soaked," he said, feeling the sweater I'd dropped over a chair. "You must have been frozen. I'll make you some tea."

He left before I could say I didn't want any tea, and as he passed the piano on his way to the kitchen, he played half a dozen notes. After a while he came back and placed the teapot beneath my nose; then he went back to the drawing room and started to play.

"It's Bach," he raised his voice above the music. "You know the one, don't you? I got some new scores in Fez, in a strange place by the Bab Boujouloud, I have the impression they sell things stolen from foreigners' villas in Casablanca, Tangier and places like that. Do you think it's possible the Moroccan police let them rob the French? They're like gods in this country."

"Who?" I said. "The police or the French?" I'd hesitated before opening my mouth. I would have preferred not to have talked to him, but the tea was hot and sweet and felt good, so good that I suddenly felt like laughing. Who would think of trafficking in stolen Bach scores in Morocco?

"Morocco is not Vienna. No one trafficks in scores here," I said.

The tea needed a few drops of something. It was raining everywhere in the country except in that room, where the wood was burning beneath the notes of a stolen score by Bach.

"Is there any of the drink left that Alcira brought from Melilla?" I shouted to make myself heard above the piano.

He appeared with a bottle of absinthe of which there was little more than three fingers left. I felt humiliated. The liquid was a marvellous golden colour which drew me. It was wonderful to hear the stream of liquor falling in the half-empty cup of tea.

"Pour it all in," he insisted. "You know I never drink. On my way back from Fez I met Charpent and spoke to him. I've got news. He said he will come to eat with us next Friday. You were right. Did you know he's quite well known as a poet in France? The French doctor at the hospital told me; because, when I saw you weren't coming back I went down to the hospital. I had the impression something bad was going to happen to us. Do you know, Rachida hasn't been coming either these past few days. . ." He was going to pieces. "The house started to frighten me. It's an eerie place. I don't think I could get used to living alone again."

He wasn't looking at me, but towards the window, towards the bare trees and the mist. The first houses of the town could barely be seen through the clouds. The wood collapsed inside the burner and the fire flared up more violently. I didn't feel like talking. The tea was finished and all that was left in the cup was the last dash of absinthe he had just served me. I drank it slowly, savouring it with my eyes closed.

When I woke up it was dark. It had stopped raining, though I could still hear the sound of the drops on the garden. Beyond the window, black clouds crossed the sky, and from time to time the moon appeared among them, like a pale flicker of flame. Someone was weeping in the drawing room. They were long, regular sobs, like those of a dog that has been punished.

I got up. Beside the window nearest to the piano, a woman was weeping as she looked through the glass towards the darkness and the distant lights. Her body was wrapped in a *gandora*, and there in the corner, weeping alone, she presented a terrible image. It was as if someone had come from very far away just to weep there. I cried out, terrified:

"Schkun. Who are you?"

She turned as she heard my cry and we stood face to face. If we had stretched out our arms, we could have touched. The sobs had suddenly ceased and now I could hear her breathing. Above the veil that covered the lower part of her face, shone two small eyes marked by a line of khol. I recognised them at once, despite the makeup.

"Francisco!" I said

I saw him run off among the trees and disappear, beneath the moon, down the slope of the ravine.

Three or four days passed before we spoke again. Rachida had returned to the house and was surprised to receive instructions to serve our meals separately. For me those were terrible days; although I'd already managed to rent a house through Hassan, I was in a state of uncertainty. Abd–el–Jaq, my close confidant at the university, had stopped talking to me for no apparent reason. I learned they had given him a post in the administration of the Spanish Department and now he was frequenting the same cafés as his Moroccan comrades, whom he had so often called traitors.

One day Francisco came into my room and stared at me. I would never have believed his eyes could be so hard. He looked at me from far above and far away, as if he had a reason that I had not even begun to intuit. He grew still taller when, before turning to shut the door, he said:

"You'll never write: you're only interested in panoramic views."

12 My last days at La Creuse were full of surprises. Abd-el-Jaq turned up unexpectedly at the house. He was carrying a spray of white Christmas flowers which he had picked on his way up. He embraced me in the doorway and stayed a long time in my room, telling me stories about his brothers and sisters, who lived just outside Mequinez. It was like the first days after we met. He asked me for some books and returned others I'd given him months before. We spoke about literature again.

At nightfall we went down to the town and revisited the brothel in the *mellah*. This time he insisted we share a girl between us and that I should be the one to choose. When he told the girl what we wanted to do, she resisted for a moment, then burst out laughing and embraced us both. We went into the room arm in arm. It was not the same one as on the first occasion; this time it was a narrow room, badly lit by a window set near the ceiling. We spent a long time with the girl. After leaving the brothel, holding hands, we headed for the bar. There, Hassan and Abd-el-Jaq watched one another in silence like two rivals. Days later Hassan said:

"C'est ridicule, ton ami. Est-ce que tu n'as pas remarqué comment il prononce le mot autobus? Toubus. C'est ridicule."

Hassan and I had laughed at Abd-el-Jaq. We bought some bottles of wine and went out into the country to drink. The afternoon was magnificent; one of the first days to give a hint of what the spring in Mimoun might be like. We baptised Abd-el-Jaq with the name "Monsieur Toubus". But by that time I had already moved into my own house.

The day Abd-el-Jaq stayed in Mimoun had ended badly. I offered to accompany him to the taxi rank and Hassan left in a sulk. Abd-el-Jaq took advantage of the moment we were alone to ask for money. It seemed his father was ill and the doctors were demanding a fabulous sum to operate on him. We had to go back from the taxi rank to La Creuse to pick up the money. I did not have much, but given the gravity of the situation I managed to get together a few hundred francs which I would never see again. Abd-el-Jaq thanked and embraced me with tears in his eyes. Months later I learned that he had pursued every Spaniard in Fez, one by one, showing them a bloodstained shoebox with a foetus inside. He told them that his girlfriend had got pregnant and there was no choice but to have an abortion. He got something out of everyone. He began to treat me affectionately again for a time, but soon started to ration his greetings once more, until at last he denied me them altogether.

Meanwhile Francisco was trying to keep me in La Creuse. He was frightened. He didn't want to be left alone again. Someone had told him that Rachida was one of the best known witches of the town, and I came to suspect that someone had told him the story about the French missionary. Not so. I myself described to him the end of that poor unfortunate and the legend surrounding La Creuse when, years later, we happened to meet in Madrid. A lot of time had gone by since those days when he tried in vain to get me to stay.

That last week he hardly left the house. He did not go up to the Marabout Café in the evening, nor did he bring back any lovers. He showed me that La Creuse could be a world, just we two, of perfect delight. He missed classes. He stayed in his room, reading, and at dinner time he would say:

"We're no trouble to one another at all, are we?"

He played the piano, put flowers in my room and spoke as if, suddenly, he had found some special peace deep inside him. But he was a tense string waiting to snap. Some nights his efforts to stay calm would collapse as he went back down to hell, from where he would call to me, sobbing:

"Don't go, Manuel. I'm afraid to be left alone here. I couldn't stand a single day of these branches scraping, all these floorboards creaking, this cursed wind of Mimoun that drives a man crazy. And the house, aren't you afraid of the house?"

To complicate matters still further, one night I heard screams coming from close by the house. At first I thought that someone might have fallen down the ravine. It was not unknown for beggars or drunks looking for shelter in one of the caves on the slopes of La Creuse to roam around the area. I went out of the house and spent a long time trying to find out where those cries were coming from, cries which were repeated the next day and for several more nights.

I began to wonder whether it was Francisco calling to me, trying to awaken my compassion at leaving him in a house that, for him, was filling itself with ghosts. Every time I heard the cries I went to Francisco's room and found him there, by the stove, absorbed in his reading. I finally had to accept that he had nothing to do with those noises. They were dreadful wails. They would start all of a sudden, be repeated three or four times, then die down for irregular periods of time, sometimes for hours. They started up soon after night fell and again in the early morning.

The day before my departure, when I had lost all hope of discovering the origin of those screams, I heard them again. At first there were three or four cries, and then a long atrocious roar which seemed it could not have been uttered by any human throat. At the other end of the space which served as a garden to the house, outlined against his window, I saw Charpent's profile. He was raising his arms to the sky, and, without ceasing to howl, was hurling objects all around him. You could hear the crash of furniture, of glass smashing on the floor. Above all you could hear his desperate cries, which turned gradually into an animal whine.

At that moment I felt long thin fingers sink themselves into my arm. It was Francisco. He too had heard the racket in the house next door that night and had come into my room. He burst into tears against my shoulder.

"Because of you that diabolical man was on the point of setting foot in my house!"

And then:

"I'm afraid. I beg you, please don't go."

13 Hassan appeared at La Creuse at the time arranged for me to move out. We loaded the suitcase with my clothes, a pair of boxes full of books and papers, and my typewriter, into his battered Citroën. Francisco didn't want to say goodbye: he got up earlier than usual and went, to the institute I suppose, without giving me the chance to exchange a single word with him. Before leaving I left a note in his room and arranged with Rachida that she would come down a couple of times a week to tidy the new house. To seal the agreement I put a few dirhams in her hand. She took them with a smile.

The house I had just rented was almost out on the plain, at the very edge of town, and had a small orchard surrounded by a white wall. It seemed to me modest but very agreeable, and I occupied it with real optimism, as if the new surroundings and independence would change my life in Mimoun. Hassan behaved that first day – and would behave in those that followed – as if we had rented the house for the two of us. He ate with me, accompanied me to the market and helped me to buy my furniture, at a good price, in the filthy courtyard of the *funduk*.

There, days later, I would buy the fine wood burner, a table built of boards from old broken fruit boxes, a pair of chairs and some wicker shelves. The rest of the furniture would comprise two foam cushions, some mats and a mattress which I lay on the floor in the room to be occupied by the table and the stove. The day of the move I only had money enough for the mattress and two blankets. I still did not imagine that I never would get to furnish that house, even though my plan at that moment was to stay there a long time.

All that year I spent in Morocco the bulbs hung naked from the ceiling; I never had enough money to acquire a carpet, and I didn't even get to buy any of the cheap copper or clay objects which decorated the other foreigners' houses. The alcohol would carry away all that might have remained of my modest teacher's salary, which was only the same as the Moroccans earned. Although I pretended not to notice it, I was seized during the first evening of my stay in the new house by a bitter sense of provisionality.

Hassan had left to sleep at his parents' home. The sun had fallen beneath the bare branches of the old elms and I had been left alone in an empty house, whose walls noted every sound and returned them instantly with a metallic echo. Until night fell it had not occurred to me that in order to live there I was going to need a mass of small objects which would have to be accumulated, little by little. I wrapped myself in the blankets, without undressing, and sat on the mattress on the floor, occupying one of the corners of the room. The light given off by the bulb was weak and yellowish, a light that seemed to spring directly from forgotten memories of childhood.

There before me, in the fragile light, was everything I owned: the shapeless heap made up of the case, the boxes, the typewriter in its cover. Beyond those few things, nothing was mine. The empty rooms, the trees and the night.

The muezzin had called to prayer and the landscape had darkened still further. In the whole of that house there was not a glass, nor a plate, nor an oven to make a fire. It was situated on a hillock from which it overlooked an old wall and above it rose the roof terraces of the suburb of Al-Manzel, which would be populated – when the good weather came – by rugs, women, children and cats, but which, that cold February evening, were empty. The wind rasped against the wall and I sat watching it from my corner, for a long time, until the shadows swallowed it completely.

"Allah Akbar!" the muezzin had shouted, and the cry had stayed trembling for a long time in the sea of shadows.

I did not know that beautiful, terrible language, and I could not have faith in any god. The muezzin's words seemed to name objects I had never seen, sentiments unknown to me. I lit a cigarette and moved my fingertips towards the flame until it burned me. I felt like a bubble floating on the sea of the night and felt that when that bubble was forced to burst it would turn into nothing. The muezzin's song described gardens to which I had no access. I was no more than a pile of half-written papers shut

away in a few damp cardboard boxes. I had underlined certain phrases in the books that were hidden
inside them, and they too were part of me. Nothing.
When the needle of life pricked the bubble, the
schoolchildren of Mimoun would trace signs on the
backs of all those sheets of paper, signs which the
person who had written on the front would never get
to decipher.

I went out into the street, for the first time. Alone,
I followed the road down between the elms towards
the town. The dry branches of winter and an empty
bubble rolling beneath the dry branches. I dined at a
kefta stall by the old wall and then drank in the bar
until they closed it.

That night, for the second time, I saw the policeman with the yellow face.

"Toujours à Mimoun?" he said, offering his hand.

As usual, inside the bar the people were shouting
and kissing. The din was almost unbearable. The
policeman was obliged to raise his voice a lot so I
could hear him. Beyond, the town was deserted. The
wind rocked the wretched light bulbs which
stretched all the way along Plantain Boulevard. At
the point where the last lights of Mimoun ended, the
world was a black sea and the anonymous corpses,
beneath the earth, infected the whole country with
their darkness: they silenced it.

"Je m'appelle Driss," said the policeman.

He invited me to a beer and asked my name,
though he must have known it from the night
before. I thought of the many afternoons he must

have sat looking at my file in his office in the commissariat. There were very few foreigners living in Mimoun, no more than half a dozen.

The policeman made me tell him my name again and repeated it three or four times, as if he wanted to learn it by heart and it was extremely complicated.

"C'est juif, n'est-ce pas?" he concluded after his memotechnic exercise.

I denied it, and through the very act of denying it, felt under suspicion. He saw it the same way.

"Oui, c'est juif," he mused. And then: "Ça va toujours avec votre copain?"

I explained that I no longer lived in La Creuse and he asked about my new abode.

"Et c'est Madrid que vous habitiez avant? Bientôt je vais vous rendre visite à votre nouvelle maison. La Creuse c'était loin, mais, maintenant, on est presque voisins. Madrid c'est bien; le Maroc aussi il est bien. On bouffe bien au Maroc, on a de très belles filles et il n'y a pas de criminels. C'est un beau pays tranquille, le Maroc."

Had I allowed him, he would have accompanied me that same night back to my house. He insisted that we walk together, but I refused with a bluntness that must have convinced him that his suspicions were correct. On my way back to the house, Francisco was waiting for me in his car, parked by the wall that ran around the orchard.

"I've brought you some things," he said. "I knew that you'd have nothing here. I've brought you knives, spoons, plates, a couple of saucepans, a cooker and some things to eat. I don't need any of this. You can give them back when it suits you."

He unloaded several boxfuls of things from the car, even a flask with hot *jarira* soup so I could eat that night. He scattered it all around the kitchen floor and left. I think he was hoping I would put on some act as prodigal son, but I didn't want to play his game, even though all those things were going to be very handy. I thanked him and went out to the car with him.

Once he had gone, I had a good cup of hot *jarira* and then made some coffee. As the water boiled in the pan, it misted up the kitchen window and the house closed in snugly upon itself, protecting me and forcing the night to change its sign.

14 I was intoxicated by the spring in Mimoun. The rainy days were followed by magnificent ones in which the sky turned purple at sunset and a perfumed vegetable exhalation rose from the earth. Life burst out in the streets and opposite the new house the roof terraces of Al-Manzel filled with women, children and cats. The first flocks of white birds crossed eagerly towards the north: it was as if the snow of Bou Iblan had exploded in a thousand pieces and spread through the blue of the sky.

I had never drunk so much. It was as though my body could not bear the happiness of those glorious days. I waited longingly for the moment when the bars would open and, from mid-morning, would begin to mix my beers with wine and pastis. It was a rare day when I didn't arrive home for dinner completely drunk. Only the alcohol calmed me, placing an isolating film between my feelings and the spring. The physical unease brought on by the drink was of no importance to me. All that counted were those journeys in Hassan's car to the nearby Atlas woods. We went round the silent shores of the lakes that opened up in the mountains, among the cedars; and we drank at the edge of the clear water, enveloped in the murmur of the frogs and the song of the birds. Bou Iblan had gradually lost its snow and sailed in the distance, like some mysterious blue ship.

In our alcoholic wanderings we sometimes came across nomadic shepherds profiting from the good weather by setting up camp in the mountains. They had come from afar, from the remote oases of the south, and looked at us with suspicion. Their children offered us mushrooms picked in the woods, small pieces of handcraft they had made themselves, or fish and birds they captured round about. They asked little for these products and stood watching us drink from some distant vantage point.

My life revolved around Hassan. And whenever I tried to mix this world with that of the Spaniards in Fez, the meeting turned into a disaster. The truth is we used to turn up drunk in Alcira's house, and it can't have been easy to deal with us. The misunderstandings were also due to the reserve the Spaniards showed to the Moroccans, the result, in large part, of long and disillusioning previous encounters. That country consumed us all.

Alcira was especially patient with me. Hassan and I would empty his very modest cellar and he would gaze at us ironically as we finished off the bottles of alcohol from Ceuta and Melilla. Our relationship had something predatory about it, though I tried to conceal this by behaving generously myself whenever I returned to the city alone.

I began to consider myself a little bit Moroccan. As if Mimoun had uncovered some forgotten space in my memory. Sometimes I had the feeling that I had lived there many years before, and I tried to reconstruct the logic of the inhabitants of that moribund town. Among the Spaniards I was obliged to adopt points of view that tore me up inside. I had the sensation that I had abandoned one continent, and that I was never going to reach the other. I was adrift.

I spent a lot of my time in the medina and its old cafés. I wandered the wretched alleyways, visited the whorehouses in the *mellah,* and spent hours at the table where Hassan and his friends played cards, enveloped in a cloud of smoke. The sound of Arab music translated feelings I was rediscovering in some forgotten part of myself and I began to make out some of the words in their conversations. I did my shopping in Derijah and smoked kif with the shopkeepers.

I returned to Hassan's house. I was no longer a suspicious stranger there. At first I was received as a special guest and then, little by little, as a member of the family. Sidi Mohammed, the father, had served in the French army and was an excellent cook. He had enlisted with the secret intention of dying and had fought as a volunteer in Indo-China, where he obtained a wound in his leg, a modest pension which enabled him to acquire some land in his native village, and the certainty that it was the will of Allah which had kept him alive. The war had made him a religious man: he went often to the mosque, carried out his prayers in private, neither smoked nor drank, and criticised hypocrites who confused religion with politics. His main preoccupation was Hassan.

He it was who first revealed to me that Hassan was a frequent liar. For months I had thought that when he left my house at night it was to return to his family. However Sidi Mohammed complained that Hassan never slept at home. Every time I tried to find out where he spent the night, he responded evasively.

Rachida also mistrusted Hassan from the beginning. Whenever they met at my house, they joked like accomplices, but the very first day, after Hassan had left, Rachida had referred to him in a disparaging tone as "ce type". From then on, to name him, she always said "ton ami", as if to make it clear that if Hassan came to the house and she received him, it was simply because I insisted and not because she wanted it. On one occasion she had murmured, "c'est un profiteur," although afterwards, she thought better of it and confined herself to saying in an energetic manner:

"Les marocains sont tous des voleurs."

15 The nightmares returned and the first sleepless nights appeared. After leaving the bar I would sleep for a couple of hours in a state of agitation, and then I would wake and be unable to close my eyes for the rest of the night. It was terrible to feel the silence of the house and the sleeping town all around me, when all that could be heard was the distant barking of the dogs.

I believe the nightmares began after my meeting with Charpent on the highway to Fez.

It was early in the evening. I was returning from class in a communal taxi and had managed to occupy the place next to the driver, which was without doubt the only seat in which it was possible to travel with any comfort at all. It was not a position I enjoyed very much, because people drove very dangerously on the highway and I had already witnessed several accidents. In one of them I had to bear the image of a dead child with its head crushed by the wheel of a truck. For that reason I had throughout the winter opted to sit in the back, though it was much more uncomfortable there; however, with the arrival of the first hot days it was unbearable to be crammed in that tiny space where the sweat of four passengers mingled together.

The taxi bumped over the innumerable holes in the road, a strident metallic clamour blared out from the radio and the sun shrank behind the car as we sped along the highway. From my privileged position I could see the fields go by, the flocks of sheep by the roadside and the rows of olive trees escaping towards the hills. It was a magnificent afternoon.

When the taxi turned into the straight stretch of road opposite Batij I thought I could make out Charpent's old yellow Renault in the distance, parked over on the verge. I'd heard nothing of him for months. Since I had moved to the new house, he had never come to visit me. It seemed strange, though it was likely that Francisco – after the events of my last night at La Creuse – had not spoken another word to him, and therefore Charpent was unaware of my new address. Yet Mimoun was not a labyrinth in which a foreigner could easily get lost. I decided to ask the taxi driver to stop by the car and continue my journey with the Frenchman.

As we came alongside the car I saw that he was alone and that his head was resting against the steering wheel, as if he'd fallen asleep. As I tried to make the taxi driver understand that I wanted to get out, I suspected that Charpent was sleeping off one of his frequent bouts of drunkenness.

I got out, to the curiosity of the other passengers, who tried to see what was happening behind them as the taxi pulled away again. The sun was hidden behind the hills and the road was suddenly empty. A gentle breeze was blowing, almost a sea breeze, rustling the leaves of the olive trees.

As I reached the car I tapped on the window but Charpent did not move. His head was resting directly against the steering wheel and his arms hung the length of his body. If I leaned across the window I could see the back of his neck and his left arm. It was not exactly the position of a drunk. I took fright at the thought that he might be dead. The silence of the evening made me shiver and I hesitated before opening the door.

When I dared to do so, his head slipped and rested against his right shoulder. A trickle of blood began to drip down his forehead and then spread over the white surface of his shirt. I wanted to scream. I turned back towards the highway. A car went by in the direction of Fez and the driver turned his head to look at me.

Charpent moved. He was breathing with difficulty and had begun to complain softly, as if he were dreaming something which evoked pleasure without passion: something like a lullaby, or an embrace with someone who no longer inspires anything more than affection. I felt that my duty was to stop the first car that passed, but I didn't do it. A battered van went by, and I positioned myself so my body would obscure that of Charpent. I realised I was afraid.

I examined the wound, pushing aside his hair. Charpent slightly changed the position of his head, as if he wanted that unknown hand to caress him. His skin was hot and he was moaning as if he were rolling around in a mountain of cotton wool.

The wound was not very deep. There were others on his face, also superficial, and his hands were bleeding and covered in scratches. He looked as if he had just come out of a fight involving unwarranted brutality, or some session of refined torture. He had begun to weep. I became aware of this because the palm of the hand with which I was propping up his head became wet. He wept in silence, without ceasing to moan gently. There did not seem too much bitterness in his weeping, nor was there anything dramatic in his expression when he opened his eyes and said:

"C'est rien."

He said it two or three times. Very softly. And he only grew anxious when I suggested that we get help from someone to accompany us back to Mimoun.

"Non. Je vous en prie. Ça non. Maintenant ça va mieux. Je vais beaucoup mieux. C'est rien. Je viens de tomber sur la route. J'étais un peu saoûl et je suis tombé."

He was lying, and he had no intention of hiding the fact that he was lying. He simply begged me to be his accomplice, because it was not convenient for any-one to find out what had happened.

"Mais il faut arriver à Mimoun, et je n'ai pas de papiers," I said.

"Je peux. Je peux conduire."

We returned to Mimoun after he had rubbed his face until the patches of dry blood had disappeared. He didn't want me to go to his house with him. He left me at the door of mine, and, before starting off in the car again, insisted:

"Il ne faut rien dire à personne."

And then, shaking my hand:

"Merci."

A few days later I found a bunch of flowers in my porch, and I believe it was Charpent who sent them. I never had the chance to find out and I think it was best that way. I saw him again on only one more occasion. We barely exchanged a few words and it didn't seem an opportune moment to ask him about the flowers, which would necessarily have reminded him of the circumstances surrounding that disagreeable encounter on the highway.

I still don't know why I started to relate Hassan's nocturnal disappearances to my encounter with Charpent. I was soon to convince myself that there was no connection between them, but just for a moment I felt they were threads of a single net, the one that was suffocating us all. Perhaps that anguish was increased by the discovery that Francisco had been right about Rachida stealing from his house. One day as she lifted the cloth covering her enormous basket, I happened to see concealed there some small objects from which Francisco would never have been parted. Curiously, the look Rachida gave me as she realised that she had been discovered, was more of menace than of fear. I too was turning into her slave, because I too – like Charpent or Francisco – had part of my life concealed.

To make things still more difficult, one afternoon when she was working at the front of the garden, Driss the policeman appeared at the house. Rachida thought I'd gone out and told him I was in Fez. And that night, when we chanced to meet in the bar and I tried to explain the misunderstanding, he gently squeezed my arm with the ends of his bony fingers and said:

"Oui. Je comprends. Vous continuez à vous cacher."

In the nights that followed the bad dreams returned. The first one I remember – which was repeated several times – was particularly depressing. I was driving a car across a deathly landscape which seemed drawn with black ink. The road zigzagged between trees and the car increased its speed on the bends, totally beyond my control, seeming not to touch the road surface; it floated above the ground and its engine – I realised this only gradually – made no sound.

On one of the curves I noticed that the car had left the asphalt and yet nothing had happened. Then it returned to its place, without ceasing to run in silence, nor registering the presence of any obstacle: at that moment I understood – I don't know how – that my journey across that strange sunless geography was taking place after my own death. That landscape, the opaque light, with no definite origin, and the silence were – precisely – death.

In the instant I obtained that disconsolate certainty, the car speeded up still more and the silence became still deeper. Then I observed that the trees that lined the road were not trees, but gigantic people wrapped in *gandoras*, men and women escorting the car like a funeral cortège. The wind stirred their black tunics and made them bang on the car windows without producing any sound at all. I was dead and running with no destination.

16 Those nightmares took up the scarce hours in which I managed to sleep.

As the summer advanced, I became used to sleepless nights. I waited for dawn with no other concern than to understand the workings of that town from which I was distancing myself once more through untold litres of alcohol. I began to search for lovers with whom to fill the long nights spent without Hassan. Through my house, from ten o'clock at night onwards, passed those who had shared my last drink, or the prostitutes I'd met on some pavement or other. Everything inside me was being broken into pieces. There were nights when half a dozen of us mingled together on my mattress. I felt like an idiot. We would lie on top of one another completely drunk and then, in the darkness of the room, we would start to search for one another cautiously, as if it mattered to any of us that the others should find out.

Sometimes we would place ourselves one after another on one of the girls we'd picked up at random; on occasion we touched one another whilst pretending not to notice. Not a few times I felt like throwing out all those people who were dirtying the few corners of myself that still remained clean. Then, the following night, I would search anxiously through the bars, and everything would be repeated.

In Mimoun, no foreigner's life could be a secret. Hassan knew about what was going on in my house. Nevertheless, he pretended not to be aware of anything. Many were the mornings he came to pick me up and drove me to the farm where he was working. There, beneath the trees, I would believe for a few hours that I could rebuild my life. The sun warmed gently, and I would read, whilst the servant would bring me tea. In those moments I believed I was recovering the purity I had pursued during my first days in Mimoun, but then the cursed night returned to ruin everything. What was to be my worst period in Mimoun had begun.

When the nocturnal visitors had disappeared and nothing remained of them but the filth, the smell and the empty bottles scattered around the floor, I would go down to an old bar called the Marrakesh Café, where I looked for distraction before dawn arrived, waiting for the rickety bus that went to the Sahara. I would spend a good while there, watching the peasants with their sackloads of undefined merchandise, the soldiers saying goodbye to the prostitutes before setting off for a distant war, of which only a muffled echo reached Mimoun.

Then I would go back to the house, looking at my watch as I climbed the road with its elm trees, hoping that time had flown away from me without my having noticed it behind my cups of coffee. Later, from my window, I would watch the sun come up, and the day would turn white, like a burned photo-graph, as the light pursued me and pushed me back to the counter of some bar.

I discovered that the only secret involved in Hassan's disappearances was a woman, and found another justification for those nights of refuge in dubious company. I no longer dared go near his parents' house at dinner time, because I was so drunk I couldn't disguise it. Sidi Mohammed had looked at me with pity on those occasions and lamented.

"Hassan n'est pas bon. Il vous laisse trop seul, monsieur Manuel."

Then, as if a sixth sense had led him to know the state I was in, Francisco made his appearance. My nerves were at breaking point and moreover he too had bad nights.

"Rachida is a thief. I've just dismissed her," he told me.

"You're mad," I replied, without quite knowing why. Perhaps because I knew that I too was doing everything wrong and I was afraid of Rachida.

I invited him to a tea but when I got back from making it in the kitchen I found that Francisco had disappeared, leaving me just a written note on the garden table. "Son of a bitch," it read.

I wondered if he was going off his head and planned an excursion to La Creuse the following day. But later the French doctor at the Mimoun hospital turned up and asked me to accompany him

urgently. I imagined that Francisco had done something stupid. The doctor was very agitated. He made
me get in his car and took the road to La Creuse.

"Vous laissez trop seul Francisco," he chided.

We were all leaving one another too alone. The
ground was boiling and the trees were covered by a
heavy coat of dust. The dogs of La Creuse sought the
shade of the acacias and the red earth of Mimoun had
turned white. Below, the town remained silent
beneath the blinding light, as though beneath a
shroud. Francisco had tried to commit suicide. They
had just pumped his stomach out in the hospital and
they had taken him back to La Creuse.

He was out of danger, though unconscious. The
doctor's wife played a piece by Schumann on the
piano which turned my stomach. My head was
aching. It was hours since I'd had a single drink, and
my nerves were on edge. Francisco's head showed
above the sheet like a religious sculpture. Everything
stank of aesthetics, while the woman persisted with
her piano playing.

"Vous prenez quelque chose?" I offered, suddenly
turning into the host, and looking in the dining-room
cupboard for something I could drink.

"Non, merci," they said, as I served myself a glass
of cheap whisky that Francisco had got from God
knows where. Then I placed myself beside the bed,
by the headboard, and started to stroke his hair as if I
loved him.

I did not love him. I didn't love anyone at that
moment. I wanted to see him dead. And to see dead

the two parts of that couple excited by a false suicide. Francisco was sleeping quietly.

"Des comprimés " explained the doctor. "Il va dormir jusqu'à demain. De toute façon, il vaudrait mieux que vous restiez ici, près de Francisco, pour voir s'il a besoin de quelque chose. Il ne faut pas le laisser trop seul."

17

I spent the week at La Creuse. It was as if, at bottom, I too needed to believe in Francisco's false suicide. He had taken the pills in a toilet at the institute, no doubt because he knew that if he had done it at La Creuse, several days might have passed before anyone would find him. For a time I devoted myself to acting as though I was looking after him. I only left his side in the rare moments when I had to go down to Fez to give my classes. I called Rachida again, making excuses for Francisco's behaviour in sacking her; and I made sure there were flowers in the convalescent's room. I listened to the piano without complaint and drank on the sly, because Francisco's hatred of alcohol had grown still fiercer.

At night I could no longer bear the imprisonment and my role in the absurd comedy, and I escaped to the town without Francisco knowing. I drank until I could no longer stand on my feet. Then I would take a taxi back to La Creuse, though it was not unusual for the taxi, before it arrived, to turn around and the driver and I would end up drinking together and spending the night in the hotel, sometimes accompanied by a prostitute. The taxi drivers knew me and were more than eager to undertake those unexpected tours. The hotel porter put no obstacles in the way of my entering accompanied, as long as I paid the toll of a bottle of wine.

One afternoon I saw Hassan's car, as he was driving in the company of Driss the policeman. I ran behind the car, watched by everyone walking along Plantain Boulevard that summer afternoon. The car didn't stop, though I'm convinced Hassan saw me waving at him. Days later, when he turned up to look for me at La Creuse, he denied having seen me.

"Où est-ce que tu étais, Manuel?" he said to me. "Je ne te trouvais pas à la maison, et j'étais très préoccupé."

He was lying. He'd brought a jug of soured milk, knowing my weakness for it, and went out of his way to be affectionate. When Francisco came into the room we were kissing and I knew I had to leave La Creuse that very afternoon, with no explanation required. I realised then that I had not come back to attend to Francisco, but to place myself under his supervision so that he could punish me.

I loaded Hassan's car up with the few things I'd brought with me. Once more, the descent down the steep road from La Creuse, this time covered by a white dust you could taste. I felt tired. Hassan stopped the car by the creek and took a bottle of "Vieux Papes" from under the seat. The first swallow of wine took the dust from my tongue. It was a rough, dark wine you could feel sinking all the way down to your stomach. As we drank, Hassan told me he was in a bad way. The woman he lived with in secret had abandoned him, and he'd had to go looking in the houses of her relatives, who were hiding her.

"Aide-moi, Manuel," he begged me. "Tous ces gens veulent me rendre fou. Ces jours passés je dormais dans la forêt, tout seul. Je ne voulais voir personne. Si quelqu'un m'avait adressé un mot, je l'aurais tué."

He had got her back, but only after paying a large sum of money, negotiated at length with the intermediaries of her family. His eyes were filled with tears when he said:

"C'est toujours pareil."

He threw the empty bottle out of the window and got out of the car to look for a second bottle of wine in the boot. The second one was even worse than the first. "Doumi." He took a swig before asking me for money.

"Je suis en faillite," he wailed.

It was the first time that I too had felt like someone's go-between. I don't believe I was mistaken, though in the following months I had to forget it in order to go on living. I offered him what I could: some francs I still had in my account and the promise that I would give him more later. He embraced me and burst into tears:

"Excuse-moi, Manuel."

I had begun to hate him. He began to sing an old Berber song, whilst he gave me little butts on the shoulder with his head and wept inconsolably. He was drunk. Some peasants went by the car and stood staring at us. Once they were well past they turned again to look. Hassan – against all Moroccan convention – had not hidden the wine bottle. He held it to his face and, from time to time, put it to my lips so I could drink too.

We went on drinking till night came. When we got home we went to bed and later he took me to a place on the edge of town where most of the houses were still unfinished, bordering on the waste land and rubbish tips that served as the gateway to the countryside. A little ditch ran in front of the house. Hassan crouched down and vomited for a long time, while I supported his head.

We went into one of those constructions which, from the outside, looked uninhabited, because no light could be seen through the window blinds. There inside, sitting under a miserable electric light in a corner of the room that doubled as a kitchen, a woman crouched. The image seemed to me pathetic and I felt immense pity for that huddled body awaiting the arrival of night.

"C'est Aixa," said Hassan, introducing me; and then he started talking to her in Berber.

The woman stretched out the tips of her fingers and raised her head.

18 The image of Aixa stretching out her hand to greet me, as her head emerged from the shadows of the kitchen, would come to me again the following day, through the words with which the policeman addressed me in the bar.

"Vous progressez au Maroc," he said to me. "Vous commencez à parler l'arabe et vous vous débrouillez bien chez les marocains."

I didn't know why, but I felt that Driss was somehow commenting on my meeting with Aixa. He had added:

"Hassan ça va? Il vous soigne toujours bien?"

I remembered Hassan's car advancing down Plantain Boulevard, with Driss sitting next to the driver and me waving to them so they would see me. The isolation of people in Mimoun was reminiscent of those huge solitary trees whose roots search for one another beneath the ground. When Aixa raised her head, I discovered that she was beautiful and realised that she was used to winning each and every day. The feelings of pity I had felt at seeing her crouched in a corner of the kitchen had turned back on myself. From that first time, we viewed one another with suspicion. It was clear we were going to hurt one another.

The three of us had eaten together; and Hassan, after making supper, had started a game which would be repeated on succeeding nights. He would push the two of us until we fell to the ground, and then he would roll to our side, throwing pillows at us. We drank, we smoked hashish and went on playing and embracing until Aixa got up to make the tea. From that instant good manners and distance returned.

They refused to let me leave when I told them it was time for me to go home. Aixa pushed me back down onto the mat and Hassan mingled Arabic and French, in indignation:

"Tu ne peux pas aller chez toi tout seul à cette heure-ci. Tu auras des problèmes."

For a moment I thought they were suggesting that we all go to bed together and I decided to stay.

Not so. They invited me to spend the night in the same room we had dined in. I remember there was a mountain goat's skull hanging from the wall and that it shone there above me all through the night. The lugubrious piece of bone stood out clearly in the darkness.

I couldn't get to sleep. I heard them fucking in the next room, and then I heard the clank of buckets in the toilet and the splash of water. They washed in turns. I heard Aixa talking in the bedroom whilst Hassan coughed in the bathroom.

I tried to escape as soon as the first rays of sunlight began to filter through the cracks in the window, but the door had been locked from the inside and the key was not in the lock. I had to stay in bed until Hassan got up. He gave me a cup of tea and made me go into his room while he got dressed. I saw Aixa's shadow in the half-light. She was sleeping naked with her face to the wall.

Hassan kissed me on the mouth at the front door and then we embraced with longing. We stayed there hugging and biting one another for a good while. The sound of our parting must have reached the room where Aixa was sleeping. However nothing moved inside the house. Outside, the light had turned from yellow to white, and the birds were no longer singing. The heat was taking over everything.

When, the following night, Driss the policeman asked me if Hassan was still looking after me properly, I felt certain that someone, from some place of hiding, had taken note of everything that had happened behind the door.

19 I had the impression that Driss the policeman lived only to keep watch over me. He installed himself at a corner of the bar and spied on the door through which I would eventually enter. With his bony yellow face, he looked like some reptile waiting for its prey. As soon as he saw me, those eyes dulled by alcohol recovered an unsuspected vitality and followed every move I made. I tried to situate myself as far along the bar from him as I could, and pretended each time not to have seen him.

He would leave me be for a good while until, suddenly, he would make his move; he would seize his glass of beer and advance towards me, edging his way through the noisy groups of men filling the place. Then it would seem as if, despite that multitude, the two of us were on our own.

"Vous ne m'aimez pas," he said as he arrived at my side. "Je le sais bien. Vous ne m'aimez pas."

He invited me to a drink and spoke of Spain. Madrid for him was a beautiful, mysterious city, and he could not understand why I had been forced to leave it. "En plus, les filles," he said, "les filles doivent être très belles là-bas. Pourquoi venir ici, à Mimoun?" It was as if he too needed to understand and, being unable to do so, had remained anchored in his suspicions.

I intuited that those suspicions had become more unbearable since I first visited Aixa's house. I had no grounds for thinking that Driss had found out about that nocturnal visit, but something inside me told me that he had; and that, for whatever unknown reason, that knowledge was the key that could close the cage into which I had just entered.

"Hassan ne vous présente pas à ses petites amies?" he said.

Each night Hassan's arrival at the bar would interrupt the policeman's interrogation. As soon as Hassan came through the doorway, that sinister man sank once more into an alcoholic lethargy from which only the conversation with me had managed to drag him. He would greet the new arrival and little by little would lose himself behind his glass of beer and the din of the bar.

Hassan and I would leave the bar to go to Aixa's house. We slept there every day. I was incapable of refusing, although I knew that I was going to suffer. I told myself that only curiosity pushed me back to that house on the edge of town, which from the outside appeared abandoned. It was horrible to take part in the same games every night.

Hassan kept a hunting dog on the roof of the building and we had got into the habit of going up there to feed him. Aixa stayed in the kitchen, and Hassan and I climbed up the narrow staircase, where we invariably kissed for a long time. On one occasion we even stood and masturbated on the landing, whilst up on the roof the dog whined excitedly because he had heard us.

I deceived myself into thinking that if I discovered the mechanisms that inspired Hassan's strange behaviour, I would eventually understand the workings of that world which was torturing me. I pretended to take Hassan as an object of analysis, but in reality I had fallen in love with him.

20 Rachida was watching me too. She had realised that I didn't go back to the house at night and took every opportunity to complain and accuse the people of Mimoun.

"Il faut faire attention aux gens de ce pays," she would say.

I don't know what she suspected, although it was obvious that her hatred of Hassan had grown fiercer. She was still working in Francisco's house, to which she returned after his suicide attempt, and it was not unusual for her to arrive with little presents he gave her for me: some book, a pot, or flowers that I didn't even see wither as they disappeared from the vase the day after Rachida put them in.

I noticed things missing from the house, but did not have the strength to confront Rachida. I knew that she robbed me as she robbed Francisco, but the house interested me less each day. I had ended up not living anywhere: I spent the day running myself ragged about the medina, ate wherever I happened to be, frequented the bars and slept in the room with the goat's skull on the wall. I had completely stopped writing. I read nothing and was incapable of finding a moment's lucidity, overwhelmed by the liquor and my longing for those hasty contacts with Hassan on the staircase to the roof, whilst the dog scratched with its claws at the door.

The town too seemed to be sleeping off the lethargy of a long drunkenness. The heat and the dust seemed to cover everything those last days of summer. The plants in the garden had withered and died and all was dry and yellow. It was as if the desert had fallen imperceptibly upon us, brought in by the burning air, and had ended up occupying everything without our even noticing. A dirty mist covered Bou Iblan, which was no longer blue and aquatic as in the distant spring, but reddish and fiery in the interminable afternoons. When the first thunderstorm broke, the dust which had been floating everywhere hardened and covered over the sick plants and houses like makeup.

During those days I saw Charpent for the last time. Rachida had mentioned his visits on several occasions. On none did he leave messages or requests. He just asked after me on the doorstep and left when Rachida said I was not in. The truth is I had meant to go up to La Creuse, but did not much relish seeing Francisco again and I was discouraged by the steep walk beneath that blazing sun which hovered above Mimoun from daybreak and from which only the beer released me.

I visited neither Francisco nor Charpent, the Spaniards in Fez had gone on vacation at the beginning of summer, and it was almost two months since the faculty had closed its doors. I lived in Mimoun as if I had gradually stripped myself of everything and was left alive with a landscape that was fading away behind the dust and the sun until it seemed no more than the unreal backdrop to a nightmare.

That was when Charpent's end came.

21 I met Charpent a few days before his death. I saw his car parked outside the door of a Jewish shopkeeper who sold liquor on Plantain Boulevard and I thought he must be inside. The car was occupied by three Moroccans: a woman who looked like a prostitute sat with her face covered, next to the empty driver's seat, and two men were watching the road from the back seat. One of them turned as he saw me enter the store.

He was a tough type, dark-skinned, with a ragged moustache that covered his mouth. I would run into him again, months later and, on that second occasion, I would realise I had to leave Morocco as soon as possible. That afternoon, in front of the Jew's store, our gazes met with such intensity that I was obliged to divert mine. There are times when such a gesture is enough to make one person hate another.

"Poor Charpent," I thought again, little knowing that on this occasion my thoughts would turn into a premonition.

I was alarmed at Charpent's fragility as he stood at the counter paying for the bottles he'd packed into a large travel bag. He smiled when he saw me and his reddened eyes lit up. The man in the car kept watching us and I thought that Charpent had looked towards him before smiling at me. Then he embraced me.

I had never known Charpent so communicative. He insisted I should visit his house as soon as possible. He needed to see me, he said. Apparently, he had written some new poems and wanted me to read them. He had good news for me.

"A la fin, le Maroc, ça sert à quelque chose," he insisted. "Ce sont les meilleurs poèmes que j'ai jamais écrits dans ma vie. On dirait que c'est un autre qui les a écrits: un petit dieu que je n'ai pas le plaisir de connaître. C'est dur ce pays, mais il finit par donner à chacun plus de ce qu'il mérite."

I promised to see him soon. Charpent had become sad as he spoke about Morocco. He gave me his hand as he said goodbye. His eyes were shining in an unusual way. He had turned them back towards the car parked at the door and hastily picked up the bag with the wine bottles in.

"Vous m'excusez. On m'attend," he apologised. And then, without changing his expression, as if he were afraid that someone might see, he said hurriedly:

"Aidez-moi, Manuel. J'ai peur. Peut-être Rilke avait raison, vous souvenez-vous?"

I would have liked to tell him to stay, but I was incapable of saying a word. He passed hurriedly in front of me and didn't even turn to look at me as he opened the car door. The man with the moustache still kept his eyes fixed on me: as if he were photographing me so as never to forget me. I heard the car engine start and the Jew's voice enquire:

"Est-ce que vous désirez quelque chose?"

I bought a couple of bottles of wine and left the place convinced that Charpent needed me and that I could do nothing for him. I didn't go to the bar that night and when Hassan turned up at my house I knew I had to say no, that I would not go and spend the night with him and Aixa. Charpent had called to me from a cage opposite mine and I had been able to do nothing because he had handed the keys to someone who looked like the man in the car. I never hated Hassan as much as I did then.

The night of the last day I saw Charpent a full red moon shone in the sky. I felt like crying, as if I already knew what was going to happen days later. Something for which Hassan too was to blame. Charpent's loneliness at the Jew's counter seemed to me a collective sin which no one was able to wash clean.

When days later Francisco appeared at my house to tell me Charpent had just hanged himself, I felt as though I was reading a news item in an old newspaper. The muezzin's voice fell slowly over Mimoun; as if the heat were cradling it for a good long while until it ended up merging with the dust of the exhausted town. The sky had become opaque months before and the silence whistled along the empty alleyways. It would have been a mistake had anyone dared to speak of justice that evening.

22

Charpent's death turned the last days of summer into a nightmare. Rachida had discovered the body, which was hanging from a rope in the centre of the drawing room in the house of the missionary's servant. The door was open and the dogs were running in and out in a state of great excitement. Rachida had shouted to Francisco and then refused to go down to the police station with him. "Nous, les marocains, on a toujours des emmerdements," she said before turning into a mysterious chameleon determined to erase herself amongst the anonymous multitudes who people the souks of the country. Rachida never again uttered a single word in French. She gave up the privileges the foreign language had bestowed on her and stayed silent until the moment the police went in to La Creuse to question her. She spoke to them in Arabic and then collected her things and left.

That midday the houses of Mimoun could not be seen from La Creuse. The town remained hidden beneath a cloak of boiling steam. Charpent's body gave off a gentle smell, which Francisco persisted in describing to me in the days that followed. Apparently it was not a strong smell, though it was clinging: like rotting water that seeped into all his pores and stayed stagnant inside his body.

"I just can't get rid of the smell," Francisco complained.

On her way back from La Creuse, Rachida passed by my house, and took advantage of my being in Fez to take with her the rags she dressed in for work and three or four objects I had vaguely promised her. She paid herself for the days still owed to her, stealing a few dirhams from the box I kept my money in.

Apart from the police, only Rachida and Francisco saw Charpent's body, which was moved that afternoon to Fez without passing through the hospital in Mimoun, where the hanged man's compatriot worked as a doctor. The next day there was a rumour that his family had sent for the body from France and had sent a large sum of money to pay the transport costs. Francisco decided that the destiny of that lifeless body was the most important thing in the world to him.

He tried to arrange a meeting with Charpent's relatives, but no one was able to give him any information about them. Not even the French consul – normally so meticulous – could give him the least indication. Nor did his compatriots know anything about Charpent's life before he settled in Morocco. The only thing Francisco managed to find out was that the part of the salary which the Ministry paid Charpent in France accumulated, each month, in a bank account in Paris to which no one else had access. Francisco focused his investigations on that bank account. Charpent had turned into an obsession for him.

Through what manoeuvres I do not know, and with the telephone as his only weapon, he managed to break the secret kept by those cold bank clerks in Paris and found out that in recent years there had been no transactions on Charpent's account. Except that on a date which coincided with the day following his death, someone had withdrawn a sum of money equivalent to that received in Fez for the cost of transporting the body.

"Seulement un chèque signé par monsieur Charpent aurait pu autoriser le remboursement," they told Francisco.

The sum disbursed by the bank in Paris had reached Fez by money order. The unknown sender had not bothered to specify where in France the body should be sent.

"Mais monsieur Charpent était déjà mort ce jour-là," Francisco insisted, unable to understand that the cheque could have been signed days before, or simply falsified. No, Charpent had paid for his own funeral after his death.

I had occasion to listen in on some of the telephone conversations Francisco made from the callbox at the Spanish Centre in Fez. I can still see him, thinner and paler than ever, his forehead beaded with sweat – though I could never understand how it could spring from that dried-up body. Fez was blazing. Everything you touched was hot: the furniture in the house, the walls, the floor. Not a single drop of water had fallen on the city for months, and it seemed to be dying beneath a white cloak of haze. Only at nightfall was the asphyxiating silence broken, though the heat went on throughout the night.

Charpent's body was waiting enclosed in a zinc coffin, sealed and guarded in a refrigerated room in the Fez morgue. I had occasion to see that macabre coffin, which was shown to Francisco and me by one of the morgue attendants following payment of a fistful of dirhams. No one was permitted to open it by breaking the seals which the police and the judge had placed on its lid. Nobody, then, could see the corpse again, despite the insistence of Francisco, who persisted in declaring that he and Rachida had observed signs of violence on the body which they found hanging from a length of rope in the house of the old missionary's servant.

"It was covered in bruises, and wounds which to me looked like burns," Francisco explained. "Charpent did not commit suicide. That morning I heard voices and music in his house."

Francisco repeated to the Spaniards in Fez the story he'd told me, did so again at the French consul's, and, worse still, added new details when he spoke to the Moroccan police. I thought, once more, that he was making a mistake and I had occasion to confirm it when, on leaving the morgue, I discovered that someone was following us along the deserted boulevards of the city.

Suddenly we had been left alone in Mimoun, despite which Francisco and I were careful not to propose living together again. In the bar I became convinced that the regular customers treated me coldly, though no one seemed to know about Charpent's death. At times I blamed my own paranoia for this conviction. Hassan was nowhere to be seen. I didn't know if I wanted to see him again, but his absence troubled me: not even his family knew what had become of him. Apparently he had gone away with Aixa and her brothers to the mountains, escaping from the heat that was suffocating us all.

Rachida had left her house too. It was as if my life in Morocco had been a play and now the performance was over, the actors had all gone. When I went to inquire about Rachida, I was received by her sister, a nervous woman whose only explanation was to say:

"Safara. She's gone away on a trip."

That same afternoon Driss the policeman turned up at my house to enquire about my relationship with Charpent. For a moment I started to think he was insinuating that I had something to do with his death. I took fright. I'd been frightened for days.

"Il vivait trop seul. Il était trop déprimé," I said.

"Alors, vous pensez qu'il avait des raisons pour se suicider," he affirmed. "C'est ça. Ici, au Maroc, il y a des étrangers qui sont tombés sur la tête. Ce n'est pas bien de dire des choses comme ça à propos de quelqu'un qui vient de mourir, mais, vous savez, le rouge, le hachish."

He explained how difficult it could be to live in a strange country, without a wife, children or relatives. Driss the policeman smelled of alcohol and seemed upset. He had begun to talk to me like a father.

"C'est difficile d'habiter entre nous sans famille. Quand il se sent seul, trop seul, loin de son pays, l'homme devient dangereux."

We were standing in my living room. Driss the policeman had rested his hand on my shoulder and moved his face close to mine. I could smell his breath which reeked of alcohol. For a moment I thought he was going to kiss me on the cheek, because our faces brushed together. Then he repeated:

". . .dangereux."

And I realised that he was threatening me.

23

Francisco collapsed when he learned that the coffin with Charpent's body in it was no longer in the morgue. His willpower faded away with Charpent's body and, what was worse, he lost the courage which had led him to say before the whole world that Charpent had been murdered. As if the outbreak of the first storms had broken the tension which had kept him in constant activity beneath the burning sun of Fez.

Those storms were like hammerings on a door. They fell on Mimoun for barely half an hour, but tore off the branches of the trees and destroyed the roofs of the most fragile houses in the medina. Later, the sun came out again, and dried the dead leaves and evaporated the water in the puddles. The air turned thick, like the aroma of the *hammam*, almost unbreathable.

Francisco had turned into a trapped animal. By now he had realised what he had said and that it had not achieved anything. No one, either in Mimoun or in Fez, had seemed to listen to his theories about the death of Charpent; nevertheless, if there were one or several murderers, they knew what Francisco thought and their hands were free to act. Either way, whether his stories were true or false, Francisco was terrified.

"Don't you see? If it was them, they'll end up making me pay."

I didn't like him coming down to my house to tell me that someone had tried to force his door at La Creuse during the night, or that he had found a burnt snake in the drawing room. I felt he was involving me in something murky that could only end badly. Sometimes I thought that he was just imagining things. At other times I was certain that he really was in danger, and that in some way he was putting me in danger too.

In the bar only Driss the policeman continued to be interested in talking to me. The rest greeted me with a nod and turned back to their glasses. If I invited someone to a drink, they just thanked me for the offer but kept their distance.

Hassan had returned from the mountains. He too seemed infected by the climate of suspicion surrounding me. It was as if everyone knew that I was suffering from some contagious disease and didn't want to tell me. Hassan drank at my side in the bar, but said goodbye at the door, without inviting me to go to Aixa's house. He avoided touching me and, when we met, he offered his hand with reluctance.

One night it seemed that everything had started to change and that it was going to be like before. Hassan was talkative again, we had a good twenty beers each, and then we bought some bottles of wine to drink back at the house. My doubts about Hassan had flown away. I wanted his friendship more than ever.

Mimoun, without him, had turned into an inferno for an interminable month.

"Je t'aime bien," I told him. "Tu es mon meilleur ami."

We staggered into my house arm in arm. We were very drunk. He closed the door and threw the catch. It was what he used to do when he wanted us to drink together and go to bed. I opened one of the bottles of wine and sat beside him. He had taken off his shirt and was humming a tune. I passed him the bottle and he drank a quarter of it in one long slow gulp. At his side I heard the sound the wine made as it went down his throat. I put my hand on his leg. He didn't move until he'd finished drinking. Then, instead of giving me back the bottle, he put it between his legs, turned and stared at me fixedly. His eyes were those of a rabid cat.

"Tu ne vas pas bien?" I asked.

He shifted on the cushion and grabbed at the bottle.

"Je vais bien. Très bien," he replied.

He was drunk. He went on humming for quite a while, still staring at me.

"Déshabille-toi," he said.

I started to take off my shirt. He stayed still. We were both naked above the waist.

"Déshabille-toi," he repeated. "Le pantalon aussi."

I started to unbutton my trousers, but I saw that Hassan was not moving.

"Et toi, tu ne vas pas te déshabiller?" I asked.

He jumped to his feet, threw himself at me and started punching me.

"Déshabille-toi. Je veux te couper les couilles, espagnol de merde. Pour qui tu m'as pris? Je ne suis pas une tapette."

I didn't have time to react. He had hit me first on the face, and then in the middle of my stomach. I doubled up with the pain, and started to vomit up the beer I had just drunk. I lost consciousness as I vomited. I only knew that, as I fell, Hassan went on punching and kicking me.

"Je ne suis pas une tapette," he kept saying.

I didn't go back to the bar. I bought bottles of wine in the Jew's store and drank them alone in the house. I scarcely ate. There were only a few days left until classes began again and I spent them trying to use alcohol so I wouldn't feel anything; but the nights were interminable and I couldn't manage to kill time by either sleeping or reading. In the early mornings, worked up by the hangovers or lack of sleep, I hated myself and smashed things in the house. No one came to clean. The floor was covered in glass, paper and rubbish. I hadn't even a centime. I couldn't even think of returning to Spain. Mimoun began to shine again, autumnal and magnificent. The leaves on the trees began to turn golden and the sky was clear. Every now and then it rained. It was no longer storms, but a rain that fell for hours at a time, making everything soft, like a womb.

One afternoon, when classes had started again in Fez, and I thought that the situation might be retrieved little by little, Francisco asked me to go up to La Creuse with him. He was terrified. Someone had hung one of the dogs by tying a length of piano wire round its neck. The town, incredible as it may seem, was more beautiful even than in the first days I had spent there. From the window at La Creuse one could see the red earth of Mimoun and the golden leaves on the trees.

24 I asked Francisco to leave Mimoun. He was caught in a trap and, indirectly, had ended up putting me in there as well. Charpent's murderers – if Charpent really had been murdered – had their nets spread all over the country: the noisy souks, the bars, the university lecture halls. I was scared, and Francisco too, even though I still couldn't understand his particular way of dealing with fear. As if he were pleading for a swift punishment, he took more risks than ever: he frequented the most ambiguous places and the worst types. He took as lovers thieves and con artists. He went back to smoking at the Marabout Café and apparently returned to La Creuse in the early morning with people who intended to black-mail him and frequently stole from him. In the morning he would be terrified at what he had done during the night and would turn up at my house to tell me how someone had threatened him or how someone else had run off at dawn with his money or some object from La Creuse.

"I'm frightened to sleep alone up there," he explained. One would have said that Francisco was condemned to death and in a hurry for the sentence to be carried out. Only punishment could restore him to peace.

The start of term had put some small measure of order back into my life. Although I carried on drinking, I had to make the effort to go into Fez several times a week to give my classes. I don't know where I got the strength to go in to Fez, but I managed not to miss a single day, even though the Spanish Department made me want to vomit. Abd-el-Jaq had turned into the favourite candidate for head and passed me in the corridors at the university without acknowledging me. He had spent the summer somewhere on the Costa del Sol and had come back disguised as a holidaymaker from Madrid.

I too wanted to leave Mimoun, but the mere idea of collecting together my books and setting off back to Madrid made me feel immensely weary. I was finally convinced by Sidi Mohammed, who came round to my house anxious that I hadn't visited him for months. He stopped in his tracks at the sight of the mess and the dirt piled up everywhere.

"Je ne peux pas vous inviter à un thé," I told him. "Il n'y a pas de thé à la maison."

There was nothing in the house but empty bottles, broken glass and piles of rubbish. I cleaned one of the mats for Sidi Mohammed to sit down on. It was months since I'd changed my sheets or washed my shirts. Everything was dirty and smelled bad. Sidi Mohammed sat gazing in silence, from his corner, at that filthy room.

"Monsieur Manuel," he said, "Hassan n'est pas bon. Il vous a laissé trop seul. Il faut que vous reveniez à notre maison. Là on vous aime bien. Vous êtes pour moi le meilleur fils qu'Allah aît voulu me donner."

He held my hand for a long time before leaving
and in the afternoon he sent two of his daughters to
clean the house, wash the clothes and prepare a *tajine*
for me. For hours I heard them moving the gear
around and when they left everything was clean and
tidy. It smelt of bleach and food. All the time they
were there, they laughed and joked. I didn't know
how to thank them when they left. I closed the door
and burst into tears. For a long time I lay sobbing on
the bed. The melancholy lights of an autumn sunset
came through the window. Then I fell asleep and
woke up stiff with cold. The window had been left
open and it had started to rain. I looked at my watch.
It was midnight. The town was sleeping, and could
even be said to be sleeping in peace. The water fell on
the grass in the garden and on the roof of the house.

I wandered beneath the rain without anguish, as if,
by soaking myself, I might commune with that silent
country. Perhaps, in some anonymous place, Charpent's body was soaking too. Death seemed to have
reconciled him with that hard land. Out there in the
rain I was certain that Charpent's body had not gone
back to France, that it never would return. He would
stay there for ever, confused for all eternity with the
red earth which had given him refuge. The children
of Mimoun would one day write incomprehensible
signs on the back of the sheets of paper on which
Charpent believed he had written the best of his life.
I thought I could hear his words in the Jew's store:

"On dirait que c'est un autre qui les a écrits: un petit
dieu que je n'ai pas le plaisir de connaître. C'est dur ce

pays, mais il finit par donner à chacun plus de ce qu'il mérite."

Strange ways of love. A little god, on whom it was raining. A hostile country, on which it was gently raining. The rain was also falling on me, permitting me a strange peace. The rain was falling on the dead ones looking towards Mecca from their anonymous graves. The muffled padding of dogs soaked by the rain.

The plantain trees along the boulevard still had all their leaves, despite the lateness of the season, and the drops of water rolled down the surface of the leaves and then fell straight into the puddles on the ground. The solitude of trees, searching for one another with their roots beneath the earth. One life was too little to compromise a whole country, or even a whole city. Geography carried out its rules: the rainy autumn of Mimoun had arrived and only I, wandering at that hour of the night, appeared to disturb it.

The next morning I went down to visit Sidi Mohammed. He rejoiced to see me enter the drawing room of his house, offered me a tea and took me gently by the hand.

"Marhababik, monsieur Manuel," he said. "Welcome."

For a long time he held my hand in his. Then he himself served me tea and sat looking at me and smiling. I picked up the glass, the spoon and the bread, and he watched me like a father watching his small son playing with a puzzle. I realised his eyes were full of tears, though he had not stopped smiling the whole time.

"Retournez en Espagne, monsieur Manuel. C'est votre pays. Vous allez me manquer beaucoup, mais allez-y."

I didn't dare to embrace him. Perhaps it was enough that he was seeing me there, in his own drawing room, drinking my glass of tea in silence. I knew now that I had to get away as soon as possible. Sidi Mohammed had just given me back my strength and I had to go before I lost it again. By the time I got back to my house I had already taken the decision. With next month's salary I would buy my return ticket and settle my debts. I would go back to Madrid. My friends would help me out until I found a job.

During the days that followed I kept on at Francisco to leave as well. In vain. He had the chance of finding another post in Tetuan, in Tangier, in the south, but he wanted to stay in Mimoun. He couldn't even listen to music any more, because his record player had been stolen; La Creuse was as much of a mess as my house had been. What could still be tying him to Mimoun? He spent the dead hours staring down the tree-lined avenue, doing absolutely nothing, and at night he went up to the café and looked for someone to share his bed. That was all his life amounted to, and yet he persisted in defending it. He too had lost his strength and no one had been able to give it back to him.

Once I had taken the decision to leave, nothing troubled me, not even the discovery that someone was going through my papers and disordering the bookshelves of the house whilst I was away in Fez; or that, one afternoon, the bathroom mirror was cracked. I felt I was already a long way from all that. Though one day I was attacked by fear again. In the morning, when I was taking a taxi from Atlas Square to the faculty, I saw the man with the moustache who was with Charpent when I met him for the last time in the Jew's store. He crossed in front of the taxi at a traffic light and stood staring at me like the first time. He had a uniform on. In the afternoon, we met again. Evidently he had waited for me to come out of the faculty. He followed me to the Atlas Café and, once inside, leaned against the bar directly opposite me. He just stood there looking at me and spat a couple of times on the floor.

25 Some time later, one evening, Mimoun was covered with smoke and foul-smelling ashes rained down on the town, blackening the house fronts and the sheets hanging up on the roofs. An enormous wall of flame hung over Mimoun for hours, and then a cloud of black smoke which could not find the strength to climb into the sky. I could see the fire from the orchard of my house. La Creuse was ablaze and the flames extended to the grove of trees surrounding it. The roofs of Al-Manzel had filled with women and children contemplating the blaze in silence. People were raising their index fingers, pointing at the house in flames and then invoking Allah. No one made a move to extinguish the fire; it was Thursday, souk day, and the animals were moving about uneasily in the *funduk* courtyard.

I don't know why I should feel surprised at the fact that no one went to La Creuse to stop the fire, when I too stayed down below, in the town, watching the flames dwarfing everything; indeed, I can say that it seemed to me so irremediable that I didn't even think of going. I looked – certainly – for the places where the view was best. I saw the flames from the orchard of my house, from the meadow where the alcoholics used to get drunk by the river, from the chaotic courtyard of the *funduk* and from the French colonial quarter, with its unkempt houses and abandoned gardens. I walked around Mimoun until sunset, when the smoke plume had died down over the ruins of La Creuse; then I decided to climb the road and searched in vain for Francisco. I found only the silence of the charred walls. It was a glorious autumn evening. Flocks of white birds flew above, heading south, and the first snow had fallen on the magnificent mass of Bou Iblan. All around La Creuse it reeked of petrol.

"Lhafia," someone said to me, as I walked back to my house. "It's been an oven all afternoon."

I collected the bare essentials and took a taxi, because that night I didn't want to sleep in Mimoun. I would never sleep there again. When I arrived at the apartment of the other Spaniards in Fez, I learned that Francisco had phoned from the police commissariat to tell them what had happened. It seems he was interrogated for hours as if he had been guilty of setting fire to the house himself. He arrived in the early morning, with his clothes torn and in a state of near hysteria. That night none of us Spaniards managed to sleep in Fez.

"It was them," sobbed Francisco. "It stank of petrol and they set fire to the grove around the house. No one came to put out the fire."

What did it matter any more? He was still intent on staying there. With nothing, but there. And all that remained for me to do was pick up my few transportable things: the books, the files, my clothes. Mimoun was as far away as a nightmare. I was safe.

That's what I thought as I collected my things and put them in boxes, to load them in Alcira's car. I didn't even say goodbye to Sidi Mohammed. I did see Hassan, though. Someone told him we were clearing the house and he turned up unexpectedly. He wanted to speak to me alone. I apologised to Alcira, who was waiting for me amid the half-filled boxes, and Hassan and I went for a ride in his car. He started to cry as soon as we were out of the town, on the road to the lakes. He brought out a bottle of wine.

"Reste ici, Manuel," he begged. "Tu es mon seul ami dans ce trou. Excuse-moi."

We drank the bottle, and then another. Hassan went on weeping, with his head against the steering wheel. Night fell.

"Je dois partir, Hassan," I said. "Alcira attend."

He started up the car, still weeping. Then, as we went past the bar, he said:

"On prend la dernière ici, comme d'habitude?"

We went into the bar. Everyone there knew I was leaving. Driss the policeman had spattered his trousers as he urinated and could hardly stand up. He kissed me on the cheek.

"Monsieur Manuel, vous nous quittez. Laissez-moi votre adresse. Peut-être vous pourriez me trouver quelque chose là-bas: un petit travail en Espagne. C'est bien l'Espagne."

He had to make an effort not to fall. He was wearing light trousers and the urine stains came up to his knee. As he spoke he spattered me with saliva. He disgusted me. I told Hassan I wanted to go.

Alcira was waiting by the house. He had sat down next to a clump of flowers and was smoking as he watched the first stars which had just appeared in the sky. It was as if he'd been there for ever and formed part of all that. As if he hadn't ever been anywhere and so was condemned to go on living. When he saw us he threw away his cigarette and said:

"Shall we go?"

He hadn't waited for us to load the boxes. He had done it himself and everything was ready. We got into the car. Before Alcira started it up Hassan put his hand through the window.

He disappeared behind the first bend in the road. He had sat on the ground and was weeping with his head between his legs. After that we passed beneath the black tunnel of plantain trees and saw the lights of Batij sloping upwards, as if a wave were carrying them off for ever. The night was clear and above the shadows of the olive trees there were millions of stars.

TRANSLATION OF
DIALOGUE IN FRENCH

p.6

"You get the best coffee in Fez in the Zanzi-Bar. I love the coffee in the Zanzi-Bar. I always have it there."

p.23

"D'you see the smallest one? The one wearing jeans? I banged her the other night. There were six of us in one room and we got through four bottles of whisky. The three girls were from the best families in Fez, and all three of them were in the nude."

p.25

"Didn't you recognise me?"

p.30

"What time will you be going back this afternoon?"

p.31

"But all that was some time ago. You might almost say that all these memories belonged to some former life which has completely vanished."

p.32

"Books, words. I don't know what on earth I'm doing here, in this miserable dump. I don't know what's keeping me here. Now, I'm sick. You know what Rilke said: 'O Lord, give unto each his own death.' I'm sure you've heard it?"

p.32

"Dogs. I hate them."

p.36

"Ah, Spain! And was it Madrid you lived in before Mimoun? You have chosen badly, monsieur."

p.38

"Leave me alone. I have no home."

p.39

"Wait till tomorrow. Tomorrow, Inshallah, you shall have some nice *jaluf* and I shall have a big, beautiful house. Would you like a big garden to go with it, princess?"

p.41

"Don't you know your pal has been looking everywhere for you? People in Morocco are too polite, you know. Even families who are too poor to take in guests keep quiet – even when they are inconvenienced. Do you know what I mean?"

p.48

"Your friend is ridiculous. Haven't you noticed the way he pronounces the word 'autobus'? Toubus. It's quite ridiculous."

p.56

"Still in Mimoun?"

"My name is Driss."

p.57

"It's Jewish, isn't it?"

"Yes, it's Jewish. Still getting on all right with your pal?"

"And it was Madrid where you lived before? I'll be making a visit to your new house soon. La Creuse was far away, but now we are almost neighbours. Madrid is great; so is Morocco. Good food, beautiful women and no criminals. It's a nice quiet country, Morocco."

p.62

"that guy', "your friend"
"he takes advantage"
"All Moroccans are thieves."

p.66
"It's nothing."

"No, please. Don't do that. It feels better now. I'm much
better. It's really nothing. I just fell over in the road. I was a
bit drunk and I fell."

"But we have to get to Mimoun and I have no documents on
me."

"It's all right. I can drive."

p.67
"You mustn't tell anyone about this."
"Thank you."

p.68
"Yes. I understand. You are still hiding yourself away."

p.72
"Hassan is behaving badly. He shouldn't leave you alone so
much, monsieur Manuel."

p.73
"You leave Francisco alone too-much."

"Would you like something to drink?"
"No, thank you."

p.74
"Pills. He will sleep until tomorrow. In any case, it would be
better for you to stay here, to be near Francisco, in case he
needs something. He shouldn't be left alone for long."

p.76
"Where were you, Manuel? I couldn't find you at the house,
and I was very worried."

p.77
"Help me, Manuel. All these people are trying to drive me mad. These past days I've been sleeping alone in the forest. I didn't want to see anyone. If anyone had spoken a word to me, I'd have killed him."

"It's always the same."

"I'm broke."

"Forgive me, Manuel."

p.78
"This is Aixa."

p.79
"You're really making progress in Morocco. You're beginning to speak Arabic and you're getting on well with Moroccans."

"What about Hassan? Is he still looking after you?"

p.80
"You can't go home at this time of night. You'll get into trouble."

p.82
"You don't like me. I know it. You don't like me."

"Then there's the women. The women must be really beautiful down there. Why come here, to Mimoun?"

p.83
"Doesn't Hassan introduce you to his girlfriends?"

p.85
"You have to watch out for the people of this country."

p.89

"Well, Morocco has its uses after all. These are the best poems I've ever written. It's as though someone else had written them: some little god I've not had the pleasure of knowing. It's a hard country, but it ends up giving everyone more than they deserve."

"Excuse me. People are waiting for me."

"Help me, Manuel. I'm afraid. Maybe Rilke was right, remember?"

p.90

"Can I help you?"

p.91

"We Moroccans always get into trouble."

p.93

"The payment could only have been authorised by a cheque signed by monsieur Charpent."

"But monsieur Charpent was already dead that day."

p.95

"He spent too much time alone. He was very depressed."

"So you think he had reasons to commit suicide? It's true. Here in Morocco some foreigners go off their heads. One shouldn't really speak ill of those who have just died, but what with wine, hashish, you know."

p.96

"It's difficult to live among us without a family. A man becomes dangerous when he feels alone, all alone, far away from his own country."

p.99

"I really like you. You are my best friend."

"Is something wrong?"

"I'm fine. Fine."

"Get undressed."

"Get undressed. Trousers as well."

p.100

"What about you? Aren't you going to get undressed?"

"Get undressed. I'd like to cut off your balls, you Spanish asshole. What do you take me for? I'm nobody's faggot."

p.103

"I can't offer you a tea. There's no tea in the house."

"Monsieur Manuel, Hassan is bad. He has left you alone too much. You must come back to our house. There you are loved. You are the best son that Allah could have wished to give me."

p.106

"Go back to Spain, monsieur Manuel. That is your country. I'm going to miss you badly, but go back."

p.110

"Stay here, Manuel. You are my only friend in this dump. Forgive me."

"I must go, Hassan. Alcira is waiting."

"Shall we have the last one here, as usual?"

"Monsieur Manuel, you are leaving us. Let me have your address. Perhaps you can find me something over there: some little job in Spain. It's good, Spain."

Founded in 1986, Serpent's Tail publishes the innovative and the challenging.

If you would like to receive a catalogue of our current publications please write to:

FREEPOST
Serpent's Tail
4 Blackstock Mews
LONDON N4 2BR

(No stamp necessary if your letter is posted in the United Kingdom.)

The Lonely Hearts Club
Raul Nuñez

'Magnificent.'   *Blitz*

'The singles scene of Barcelona's lonely low life.
Sweet and seedy.'   *Elle*

'A celebration of the wit and squalor of Barcelona's
mean streets.'   *City Limits*

'This tough and funny story of low life in Barcelona
manages to convey the immense charm of that city
without once mentioning Gaudi. . . . A story of
striking freshness, all the fresher for being so casually
conveyed.'   *The Independent*

'A sardonic view of human relations . . .'

The Guardian

'Threatens to do for Barcelona what *No Mean City*
once did for Glasgow.'   *Glasgow Herald*

'A funny low life novel of Barcelona.'   *The Times*

Also published by Serpent's Tail

Landscapes After the Battle
Juan Goytisolo

'Juan Goytisolo is one of the most rigorous and original contemporary writers. His books are a strange mixture of pitiless autobiography, the debunking of mythologies and conformist fetishes, passionate exploration of the periphery of the West – in particular of the Arab world which he knows intimately – and audacious linguistic experiment. All these qualities feature in *Landscapes After the Battle*, an unsettling, apocalyptic work, splendidly translated by Helen Lane.'   MARIO VARGAS LLOSA

'*Landscapes After the Battle* . . . a cratered terrain littered with obscenities and linguistic violence, an assault on "good taste" and the reader's notions of what a novel should be.'   *The Observer*

'Fierce, highly unpleasant and very funny.'
The Guardian

'A short, exhilarating tour of the emergence of pop culture, sexual liberation and ethnic militancy.'
New Statesman

'Helen Lane's rendering reads beautifully, capturing the whimsicality and rhythms of the Spanish without sacrificing accuracy, but rightly branching out where literal translation simply does not work.'
Times Literary Supplement